NURSE

Mr Blake van Reenen, senior neuro-surgeon at County General, is so cold-blooded that it's rumoured he has formaldehyde in his veins. So if anyone can melt his hard heart it must be fiery Irish Staff Nurse Melissa O'Brien . . .

NURSE ON NEURO

BY
ANN JENNINGS

MILLS & BOON LIMITED
15–16 BROOK'S MEWS
LONDON W1A 1DR

First published in Great Britain 1984
by Mills & Boon Limited

© Ann Jennings 1984

Australian copyright 1984
Philippine copyright 1984
This edition 1984

ISBN 0 263 74888 X

Set in 10 on 12 pt Linotron Times
03/1284/51,000

Photoset by Rowland Phototypesetting Ltd
Bury St Edmunds, Suffolk
Made and printed in Great Britain by
Richard Clay (The Chaucer Press) Ltd
Bungay, Suffolk

CHAPTER ONE

MELISSA O'BRIEN moved silently around the ward, smoothing a bed-cover here, rearranging some flowers there. Then, standing back, she surveyed her handi-work.

'Nurse,' called Mrs Betts from her bed by the window, 'can I have a drink?'

'Of course,' said Melissa as she went across to her immediately. The woman had recently had a tumour operated on, and now the bandages had been removed she was wearing a little cotton skull-cap. Melissa poured the water out into a glass and gently propped Mrs Betts up more comfortably with an extra pillow.

'There, can you manage, or do you want me to hold it for you?' she asked.

Mrs Betts smiled gratefully. 'Let me try, Nurse. I've got to start doing things again for myself. But you will stay won't you?' she asked anxiously. 'In case I drop the glass.'

'Of course I'll stay,' Melissa smiled encouragingly. 'But I'm sure you'll manage just fine.'

Mrs Betts did manage, but with a great deal of diffi-culty. Although the tumour had been removed she still had great problems in co-ordinating the movement of her hands.

'Mr van Reenen says I should get almost complete movement back,' she told Melissa. Then she added,

'You're new on this ward, aren't you? Do you know Mr van Reenen?'

Melissa shook her head. 'No, I don't actually know him, but I understand he is a very good neurosurgeon.'

Mrs Betts smiled as Melissa helped her to slip back down comfortably between the sheets. 'If I hadn't got all my hair shaved off and if I was twenty years younger, I'd be after that man!' She sighed drowsily. 'He's so gorgeous!'

Melissa smiled. From all the reports she had heard, he was far from gorgeous. In fact she had heard he was a real terror. A perfectionist to the point of being a fanatic, and woe betide anyone who didn't match up to his standards!

Mrs Betts drifted back into a half-sleep and Melissa looked around. Sister was busy writing at her desk far away at the other end of the ward. Everything was so quiet—in fact unnaturally quiet for ten o'clock in the morning. There was nothing else to do for the moment, for everything had been done. All the patients who were well enough were reading, most of them rustling the morning papers, and the others were dozing.

Melissa wandered over to the window and looked out longingly, a shaft of sunlight illuminating her gleaming chestnut hair, which was pulled back severely into a bun. She was a tall girl, five foot seven at least, and had grown very accustomed to being as tall, if not taller, than most of the men she met. The tight-fitting blue check uniform with its wide buckled belt accentuated her slender, willowy frame. From her Irish forebears she had been blessed with a flawless cream complexion, a classic oval face with a neatly chiselled nose and a wide, sensuous mouth. Her sea-green eyes were fringed with black lashes framed by delicately arched brows. She had often been told she should have been a model but had preferred to take up nursing as a career instead.

Today, however, she was feeling a little restless. It was a beautifully cold, frosty winter's day outside, and from where she stood in the stuffy, centrally-heated hospital ward, five storeys up in the air, the outside world looked very desirable indeed. It was her first day on the neurosurgical ward as staff nurse and she had expected it to be exciting, not quite the way it was.

Looking down at the grass and trees far below, sparkling in the sunshine, she sighed a long, drawn-out sigh.

'Are you practising deep breathing, or do you normally make a noise like that?' a deep, cynical voice enquired.

Melissa swung round to find a pair of hooded grey eyes observing her disapprovingly in a way that sent shivers through her. The tall, muscular figure before her exuded a force of masculinity and disapproval, both of which were impossible to ignore. He was wearing a crisp white coat over a well cut suit. She assumed he must be a doctor, but even so she felt slightly annoyed. What right had he to look so damned disapproving? Melissa opened her mouth to reply, but he interrupted her.

'Don't bother me with ridiculous apologies, just get on the ward round and be smart about it.'

Melissa's hot Irish temper began to boil. Who the hell did he think he was? She didn't mind being told what to do, but she was not going to be pushed around by some rude, arrogant stranger. Probably a newly-appointed senior registrar, throwing his weight around, she thought scornfully.

'I don't know who you are and I couldn't care less,' she

hissed at him. She wanted to shout, but that was impossible because of the proximity of the patients. 'You have
no right to tell me what to do.'

'I am Blake van Reenen,' he said, his dark face totally
devoid of expression, although there was just a hint of a
smile tugging at the corners of his stern mouth. 'I am the
senior neurosurgeon and head of the Neurological Unit.
I organise a teaching ward round every Monday morning, starting at ten o'clock, and that is where you should
be, waiting with everyone else for me to start.' He
paused for a moment. 'Or perhaps you think you don't
need the benefit of my expertise!' The last remark was
uttered in a cutting tone of voice.

Melissa gasped in horrified dismay. Now she recognised him, although only by his name, for she had never
seen him before. She suddenly realised why everything
had been prepared and finished early, and why all the
other nurses had disappeared, except Sister. But why
had nobody told her? Her cheeks flushed brilliant
crimson under his piercing gaze.

'I'm sorry,' she stammered. 'I . . . I didn't know I was
supposed to go on a ward round.'

'Well, you do now,' was all he said.

Melissa didn't wait to be told a second time but dashed
out of the ward, crashing into the doorway on her way
out.

'Careful, Nurse!' she heard his mocking laugh. 'We
don't want you to be a casualty on your first day with us.'

Luckily she found the others, about ten people in all,
assembled on the floor below. She tacked herself on to
the group of nurses and junior doctors, and whispered to
Charlie, an anaesthetist, who was a special friend of
hers,

'Why didn't you tell me, or get someone else to tell me that I should have been on the ward round?'

'Sorry,' whispered back Charlie. 'I just assumed that you knew.'

'Well I didn't,' said Melissa crossly, 'and then this wretched man came and . . .'

'When you've quite finished your conversation, Nurse, perhaps I'll be allowed to get on with the teaching.' The sarcastic voice of Blake van Reenen came ringing across the room.

Melissa flushed crimson again and tried to lose herself at the back of the crowd. Mercifully she managed to keep herself well to the rear of the round for most of the time. From her viewpoint at the back she felt sorry for the junior doctors and nurses unlucky enough to be standing at the front, nearest to Blake van Reenen. If they couldn't answer one of his searching questions they were scathingly exposed in front of the others. Although, to be fair to Mr van Reenen, Melissa had to admit that most of the questions he asked they should have been able to answer. It seemed, however, that he struck most of them dumb with fear!

They had almost reached the end of the ward round now and Mr van Reenen was introducing the last patient. Melissa had noticed right at the beginning of the round that when he spoke to patients he seemed to change. His voice was low and gentle and he smiled at them reassuringly. He turned to everyone.

'Now, this is Mrs Smith,' he said, indicating the middle-aged lady in bed. 'I'm going to ask one of you to try to read her scan pictures and diagnose her illness. Mrs Smith already knows what she had the matter with her, so you can speak out.'

Bending down he took a series of scan pictures from the folder at the side of her bed. As he did so, Charlie gave a sigh and said to Melissa 'I've got a horrible feeling it's going to be my turn now. He hasn't asked me anything yet.'

Blake van Reenen's grey eyes looked around the room and came to rest in their direction.

'Oh well, keep your fingers crossed for me,' said Charlie, and thrust something quickly into Melissa's hand. She had just time to realise that it felt wet and sticky and somehow alive, when Blake van Reenen's voice said,

'Dr Cook, come and look at these scans. Oh, and you too, Nurse,' to Melissa. 'Let's see what you know.'

Melissa followed Charlie through the crowd, less worried now about Blake van Reenen than the object she was unwillingly holding in her hand. What on earth had Charlie given her? He was renowned as the practical joker of the County General Hospital, she knew that, but surely he wouldn't play a prank on her now?

Charlie picked up one of the scans, which showed a vertical slice of the patient's brain and, holding it up, said, 'This shows a well-defined, dense heterogeneous opacity in the right frontal region, which has been enhanced with constrast medium and is displacing the right lateral ventricle to the left.'

'Very good,' said Blake van Reenen looking surprised. And then to Melissa, 'And now, Nurse, can you give us a diagnosis?'

'A meningioma,' gasped Melissa desperately. The thing in her hand was alive, she was sure. She could feel it squirm. She had to go and get rid of it before she screamed.

'Excellent, Nurse,' she vaguely heard Mr van Reenen's voice as she tried to control herself. 'It is a little unfair of me asking a new nurse, but you did well.'

He turned back to speak to the patient and Melissa tried to squeeze through the crowd and get out of the ward, but she couldn't manage to get through the crush.

'The ward round is now over,' she heard Blake van Reenen say. 'Thank you, ladies and gentlemen.'

The group of junior doctors, nurses and physiotherapists started to walk slowly out through the double doors at the end of the ward. Melissa began to push her way through and had just reached the doors when the thing in her hand seemed to give an extra-vigorous squirm. With a little scream which she just couldn't suppress, Melissa opened her hand and a bright, sickly green-coloured rubber frog flew out and landed *splat* on the polished floor of the ward.

It was made of a jellyish sort of rubber and had a metal spring inside it and Melissa realised that was what had made it seem to move in her hand. She wished now she had been braver and had held on to the damn thing!

The other girls in the group screamed and leaped away from the offending object and for a few seconds pandemonium reigned. That was, until Mr Blake van Reenen came on the scene.

'What is the meaning of this disgraceful rumpus?' he grated. 'This is a hospital ward, not Battersea Fun Fair!' He spied the green frog on the floor and bent down to look at it. As he did so, the spring inside it activated again and it jumped into the air.

'Whose stupid idea of a joke was this?' he asked in a voice like ice.

Melissa could see Charlie standing behind Mr van

Reenen, desperately shaking his head at her. She knew
he had already been in serious trouble with his boss, Dr
Gilbert, the senior neuro anaesthetist, for switching
name-tags on everyone's theatre boots, and she felt
loathe to land him in the soup again, even though he
deserved it.

Steeling herself, she went forward and picked up the
revolting rubber creature. 'I'm sorry, Mr van Reenen,'
she said hastily, 'I . . .' She racked her brains for a
plausible sort of reason. 'It was in my pocket and the
spring must have gone off.'

He looked at her suspiciously, his grey eyes dark with
displeasure. 'Do you usually carry rubber frogs around
in your uniform pocket?'

Melissa tried to smile in a composed fashion, but her
facial muscles seemed paralysed. 'I bought it for my,
er . . .'

'Little brother,' interrupted Charlie helpfully.

Melissa shot him a baleful look. She could do without
his help! He had got her into this mess in the first place,
and besides, she didn't have a little brother, although, to
all intents and purposes, it looked as if she would need to
have one for the moment.

'Yes, my little brother,' she agreed, and putting the
offending frog in her pocket walked out of the ward
swiftly, before either Charlie or Blake van Reenen could
say anything more.

Later that day in the canteen, plodding through the
mundane hospital fare, Melissa was teased unmercifully
by the other girls from the neuro ward.

'I just loved the expression on his face when he bent
down and the little green thing jumped up at him,' said
Di. 'Do you know, for one awful moment I thought he

was actually going to smile!'

'Yes, that would have been quite something,' agreed Rosie. 'We should really have had to mark that day on the calendar.'

'He smiles at the patients,' said Melissa, 'and I think he was quite justified in being angry with me. After all, it was a stupid thing for me to do.'

'Hey!' said Rosie. 'Why are you defending him? Do you fancy him or something?'

'Don't be ridiculous,' answered Melissa. 'I don't even know the man. I met him today for the first time and already I've managed to get two black marks. I was late for the ward round and then I dropped a green rubber frog on the floor!' She laughed. 'If I fancied the man I can think of better ways to get his attention. Anyway,' she added, 'what's so wrong with him that you all dislike him?'

'It's not so much what's wrong with him,' said Di. 'Everyone admires him—he's one of the best neuro-surgeons in the country. It's just that . . .'

'Well, go on,' said Melissa. 'Don't keep me in suspense, for goodness' sake!'

'Well,' said Di. 'He has no sense of humour, and as far as we know he never has girlfriends.'

'Well, if he *does* he keeps it jolly quiet,' interrupted Kate from the other end of the table. 'I think he's cold-blooded.'

'And,' added Di dramatically, 'if he cut himself he wouldn't bleed. That man has not got normal hot blood in his veins!'

Melissa raised her dark eyebrows expressively. 'What theory have you got? What *does* he have running through his veins then?'

'Probably formaldehyde,' said Di.

'We can tell you've just finished a course in pathology,' said one of the other girls sarcastically.

'Well, I don't care what he's like as a man,' said Melissa firmly. 'If he's kind to the patients and is a clever surgeon, that's good enough for me. There's only one thing,' she added thoughtfully.

'What's that?' asked Di.

'I think it would be just as well if I keep out of his way for a bit. I'll try to make myself invisible when he comes on the ward.'

'That will be impossible, you gorgeous redhead, you,' said a teasing voice behind her.

Melissa turned. It was Charlie Cook. '*You!*' she exploded. 'I could cheerfully strangle you! Whatever did you do such a rotten thing for? And don't call me a redhead!' she added.

Charlie threw up his hands in a defensive gesture. 'Sorry, you gorgeous thing! No, don't hit me, don't hit me!' he pleaded in mock dread.

He sat down with the girls at the table. 'I know you're never going to believe this, Melissa, but I had that frog in my hand intending to play a joke on Chris—you know, the new senior house officer in neurology. But I forgot to put it away before the ward round. I was late too,' he added by way of explanation, 'and didn't want to get another rocket.'

He smiled at Melissa beseechingly. 'When I saw that van Reenen was going to get me to hold those scan pictures up I had to get rid of it quickly and you just happened to be the nearest person.'

Melissa glowered at him, but couldn't keep up her anger for long as he pulled a comical face at her.

'No wonder you're called Crazy Charlie around this place,' she said. 'I suppose one day you'll grow up and turn into a serious doctor.'

'Not if I can help it,' said Charlie. 'You know I'm serious about the patients, but I'm never going to be a van Reenen of this world.'

'I should hope not,' said Rosie. 'We all like you just the way you are.'

Charlie was very popular with all the girls. He was a fun-loving, gregarious type and there wasn't an ounce of malice in him.

'Anyway,' said Charlie, addressing Melissa, 'I'll make it up to you as soon as I've got my new car. How about that! I'm negotiating for a white MG and when I've got it I'll take you out in it for a spin.'

'Thanks a lot,' said Melissa laughing. 'It's about time you changed that heap of rust you drive around in. I'm glad to hear you're investing in a decent car.'

'Who said anything about it being decent?' replied Charlie. 'It needs a bit of work on it. There are a few holes I thought I could patch up with plaster of Paris, it being white, you know!'

'That means it's dropping to bits,' said Di, getting up to take her tray back to the hatch. 'I should be very careful of that offer if I were you, Melissa.'

'I will, don't worry,' replied Melissa, also rising. 'Ah well, back to work now. Let's hope I don't bump into Blake van Reenen again today!'

Back on the ward, Sister put her to work to bath Mrs Smith. It was to be her first proper bath since she had been in hospital and she was looking forward to it.

'I'm sure I can manage on my own, Nurse,' she said as Melissa helped her undress.

'Well, Sister is equally sure you can't, and anyway, we can't have all the good work undone by you slipping on the bathroom floor, can we?' said Melissa firmly.

Mrs Smith did need more of a hand than she thought, as she had been in bed for so long her balance was very precarious. And anyway, the removal of the tumour, although successful, had left her with a slight hemiplegia. Melissa found it hard work, and by the time she was finished she was hot and flushed with the exertion. Her normally neat hair was damp and long tendrils had escaped from the bun and were feathering down the sides of her face.

Mrs Smith had found it tougher going than she had expected, too. 'I didn't know I was going to feel so weak, Nurse,' she puffed. 'I feel so strong when I'm just lying there in bed!'

Melissa helped her back into bed and gently tucked her in. 'You must remember,' she said comfortingly, 'that you've had very serious surgery. You mustn't try to run before you can walk.'

Mrs Smith smiled. 'You're a good girl.'

'Now I'll pop along to the ward kitchen and make you a nice cup of tea as we have missed the tea-trolley, and then after that you can have a little snooze before supper.'

'That will be lovely,' said Mrs Smith gratefully.

Melissa went across to Sister's desk before going to the kitchen, which was at the far end of the ward. 'Is it OK if I make Mrs Smith a cup of tea?' she asked.

Sister Moffat looked up. 'Yes, of course,' she said. 'And while you are doing that you can make a pot for Mr van Reenen. He's on his way up to have another look at

Mrs Betts, and I know he has been closetted in theatre since the ward round this morning. He'll be grateful for tea and biscuits, I'm sure.'

'Yes, Sister,' said Melissa. She sped down the ward to the kitchen. Hell, she didn't want to have to see Blake van Reenen again, not today. She wanted to give him time to forget about a stupid nurse who let green frogs loose on the ward! Oh well, she thought resignedly, if I hurry perhaps I can do it and get out of the way before he comes up to the ward.

She put on the kettle and got out the teapot for Mr van Reenen, then a nice bone china cup and saucer with matching sugar bowl and milk jug, arranging it all on a small tray with a plate of Bourbon biscuits.

For Mrs Smith she got out the normal hospital issue of a plain white cup and saucer. The kettle boiled and she made the tea. Quickly she poured out Mrs Smith's and put some biscuits aside for her as well.

I'll take her tea and biscuits down now, Melissa thought. Then I'll dash back and leave the tray ready here in the kitchen for Mr van Reenen. Then I'll make myself scarce!

After making sure that Mrs Smith had her tea on the bedside locker within easy reach, Melissa dashed back down to the kitchen. She topped up the teapot with boiling water and set everything out in readiness on the small table in the kitchen. She was about to leave when Blake van Reenen came in.

'Oh, Sister told me I'd find you here, and that you had kindly agreed to make some tea for me.' His firm, cool voice was expressionless, and his heavy-lidded grey eyes gave nothing away. He made Melissa feel uncomfortable and she was suddenly aware that her hair was still

damp from bathing Mrs Smith and that strands of it were
hanging about her face.

Blake van Reenen obviously noticed it as well, and
raised his dark eyebrows. 'You look as if you have been
pulled through a hedge backwards, Nurse,' he remarked
coolly.

Melissa felt herself blushing. She pushed the offending hair behind her ears. 'I've been bathing Mrs Smith,'
she said stiffly, 'and I haven't had time to tidy myself up
since.'

'Ah, Mrs Smith,' he said. 'She is quite a large lady.
Did you manage her by yourself?'

'Yes, I did,' snapped Melissa, annoyed that he was
perhaps implying that she couldn't manage on her
own.

'Then I think you deserve a cup of tea as well, Nurse.
Perhaps you would like to have one with me? Keep me
company.' His suggestion filled Melissa with surprise
and apprehension.

'Well, I don't know,' she stammered. 'Sister might
have something for me to do.'

'Sister knows. She suggested it as, apparently, you
missed tea this afternoon, like me.' He perched easily on
the edge of the table. 'Will you pour, or shall I?'

'I'll pour if you like, sir,' muttered Melissa, cursing
Sister Moffat for putting her in this predicament. She got
out another cup from the cupboard and started to pour
out the tea. His presence made her nervous. She felt all
fingers and thumbs.

'Thank you.' He took the cup from her and helped
himself to a Bourbon biscuit. 'You are new here, aren't
you?'

'Yes,' answered Melissa, leaning back nervously

against the cupboard, trying to put as great a distance as possible between them.

He laughed suddenly and his eyes seemed to lighten as they sparkled with amusement. 'I'm not going to bite you, Nurse. You can come and sit down beside me.'

There was nothing for it but to do as he suggested, thought Melissa. It would look so rude if she didn't. She sat down self-consciously in the chair by the table. He remained where he was, perched on the table-top, looking down at her.

'Where did you come from?' he asked suddenly.

'Where?' Melissa hesitated. 'Do you mean before I came to the neurosurgical ward? Well, I was on Casualty for a spell, and before that Men's Surgical. Of course, I've been almost everywhere in the County General—I trained here.'

'Oh, I see,' he said slowly. 'Then I'm surprised I haven't seen you before.'

'Consultants and junior nurses' paths don't often cross,' said Melissa. 'Remember, you haven't been here long and I didn't know who you were either.'

He smiled again. 'No, I remember now. You told me you didn't know who I was and couldn't care less. I *think* those were the words you used.'

Melissa felt her cheeks burning. His voice sounded amused and she didn't dare look up and meet those inscrutable grey eyes. 'I wouldn't have snapped back at you if I had known who you were,' she said lamely.

'I suspect you have a temper to match that red hair of yours,' he said.

'It's not red, it's chestnut,' retorted Melissa. If there was one thing guaranteed to get her riled, it was the suggestion that her hair was red. Charlie Cook always called her a redhead purposely to annoy her. She wasn't going to have one of the consultants getting in on the act as well! She flashed him an angry look from her green-flecked eyes.

He put down his cup on the tray. 'Red or chestnut, it's a very pretty colour anyway.' Reaching forward, he lightly picked a wayward strand between his fingers and tucked it gently behind her small ear.

Melissa was startled to find that the touch of his hand sent such a strange tingle down her spine. For someone who had the reputation of being cold-blooded, he managed to send sensual vibrations through her very easily indeed, she thought, feeling even more confused. She could feel a hot pink stain creeping over her cheeks.

'I must go now,' she said quickly, and replaced her own cup on the tray. 'I'd better wash up, otherwise Sister will be after me.'

'I'll help,' he said, coming to stand beside her.

'No, no,' said Melissa quickly, anxious to rid herself of his disturbing presence in the kitchen. 'You've got to go and see Mrs Betts, haven't you?'

'No hurry,' he replied coolly, picking up a tea-towel from the small radiator in the kitchen. 'It's quite restful here with you. Makes a pleasant change from peering into people's brains!' He sighed. 'And it puts off the moment when I've got to tell Mrs Betts that she has to go back to theatre.'

Melissa turned and looked at him. He didn't look cold-blooded at all. Just a tired and anxious man. Instinctively she put out a tentative hand and touched his arm.

'Poor Mrs Betts,' she said softly. 'Are you going to take her back to theatre tonight?'

'Yes, I'm afraid we'll have to. She has another haema-toma.' He reached across with his other hand and lightly took hers. His hand was large, with long, sensitive fingers, and as he touched her Melissa felt that same tingle flicker down her spine to lodge in the pit of her stomach.

'What's your name?' he asked.

'Nurse O'Brien,' whispered Melissa, mesmerised by his hooded grey eyes.

'I meant your other name,' he said slowly in a deep, warm voice.

'It's Melissa.'

'Melissa,' he repeated, giving her name an intimate ring as he rolled it around his tongue. 'Melissa, you are making my new coat wet!'

'Oh!' Startled, Melissa snatched her hand back from his sleeve. She had indeed made his white coat wet; she had completely forgotten that her hand was covered in washing-up suds.

'Oh, I'm sorry,' she murmured. 'I always seem to do something stupid when you are around!'

He gave a deep laugh. 'That wasn't stupid. I know I've got the reputation for being a hard-hearted, cold-blooded man, but I'm not averse to a pretty girl putting her hand on my arm!'

'Oh, well—yes,' the words came out in a jumbled fashion. He had completely thrown her now. Rosie's words came back to her. *Do you fancy him or something!* This was all getting too ridiculous! Was he flirting a little with her or was she misreading the situation completely? All she knew for certain was that she had to get out of his presence before she did something disastrous, like drop-ping all the china on the floor.

With lightning speed, she packed the cups, saucers and tray away.

'I must get back on to the ward now,' she said briefly, and hurried down the corridor as fast as she could without actually breaking into a full-scale gallop, aware all the time that he was standing in the doorway of the little ward kitchen, watching her retreating figure.

Luckily, Sister sent her off straight away with one of the other girls to do the drugs round. That would be her last task before going off duty. They made their way round the ward, stopping at each patient, ticking off the various drugs they had on their charts, then cross-checking as they were administered. Out of the corner of her eye, Melissa could see Blake van Reenen sitting with Mrs Betts, holding her hand. Her heart lurched at the sight of him, remembering how she had felt when he had held her soapy hand. Don't be ridiculous, she told herself, and concentrated on the drugs round.

Eventually they arrived at Mrs Betts' bed. The notice *Nil by mouth* was hanging over her bed, so Melissa knew for certain she was going to theatre that night. As they arrived, Blake van Reenen rose from the bedside.

'As soon as you have finished,' he spoke to Melissa, 'would you draw the curtains and stay with her? The anaesthetist will be up in a few moments to look at her and write her up for a mild premed. I'd be grateful if you could stay with Mrs Betts and accompany her when she comes down to theatre.' He started to leave. 'I have spoken to Sister about it.'

'Yes, of course.' Melissa gave Mrs Betts a reassuring smile. Poor woman, she thought sadly. I wonder if she is going to pull through all this?

Lucy and Melissa finished the drugs round and Blake

van Reenen walked out of the ward past them, without a further glance. It is almost as if I imagined that little scene in the kitchen, thought Melissa, watching him.

She had to admit he was dishy in an unapproachable sort of way. Tall, very tall, with dark hair just faintly tinged at the temples with silver. But it added rather than detracted from his attraction. His face was handsome but had a proud, formidable air, probably due, Melissa thought, to his high cheek-bones and the determined line of his clear-cut jaw. His skin was quite tanned, as if he had been in the sun very recently.

She decided that the only reason that every nurse in the hospital, or every woman he met, for that matter, wasn't running after him was that he had that slightly off-putting, stern air about him.

She watched him walk the entire length of the long ward. He walked with the lithe, springing gait of a young, athletic man, and yet she thought he must be at least thirty-seven or thirty-eight.

'Hey, are you going to stand there day-dreaming for ever?' Lucy's voice brought her back to earth with a bump.

Melissa jumped, 'Oh, no! I don't know what's the matter with me, I must be tired.'

'Don't forget Mrs Betts,' reminded Lucy. 'By the time you've taken her down to theatre it should be time for you to go off duty. In fact you'll probably be late.'

'Yes,' sighed Melissa, her wandering thoughts returning to Mrs Betts. 'I'll go to her now.'

She drew the curtains around Mrs Betts' bed and undressed her gently and put on the theatre gown, carefully tying the tapes at the back. Then she sat with her and held her hand. There was very little else she

could do while they waited for the anaesthetist to make
his pre-operative assessment. Mrs Betts was very
apprehensive and Melissa did her best to reassure her,
but the woman was no fool and knew very well the
serious nature of her illness.

'I just thank my good fortune that I'm being looked
after by Mr van Reenen,' she whispered.

'Yes,' agreed Melissa. 'You certainly couldn't have
anyone better to look after you.'

The anaesthetist came—it was Dr Gilbert, the senior
consultant anaesthetist, an abrupt, pernickety little
man. Melissa could well see that he would most definitely not appreciate Charlie's crazy sense of humour. He
quickly examined Mrs Betts in a matter of fact way and
gave her a mild premed as it would not be long before
she was in theatre.

'The next time I see you will be in the anaesthetic
room,' he said to Mrs Betts briskly. 'Now, try not to
worry.' Although he was abrupt in his manner he was
kind, but Melissa could see he didn't generate the same
kind of charisma that Blake van Reenen did for his
patients.

About a quarter of an hour later the porters came to
take Mrs Betts down to theatre. Melissa picked up the
notes and tucked the blanket round the patient carefully, once she had been moved on to the trolley. Then
off they went. Melissa accompanied her charge into the
anaesthetic room where Dr Gilbert and Charlie, who
was acting as his assistant, were waiting. Blake van
Reenen came through into the anaesthetic room before
he scrubbed up.

'Thank you, Nurse,' he said courteously, his voice
cool and detached, nodding his head in a dismissive

gesture. As Melissa pushed through the double doors of the anaesthetic room into the corridor outside, she heard his low voice speaking to Mrs Betts in warm tones, gently explaining to her again what was going to happen during the operation.

For some reason she couldn't explain rationally, Melissa felt almost hurt that he hadn't spoken to her in that warm tone of voice. Stop being stupid, she told herself. Just because he was pleasant to you when you gave him a cup of tea doesn't mean that an important man like Blake van Reenen is going to think twice about some red-haired nurse who drops rubber frogs on the floor!

Lucy had been right, she thought as she trudged laboriously up the three flights from theatre to ward level. She *was* going to be late going off duty. She always made herself walk up and down stairs whenever possible. It was one way of keeping fit. Although anyone looking at her slender, shapely figure would have thought that she was very fit indeed. But Melissa was always conscious that she was a few years older than most of the girls at her level of nursing and felt in some illogical way that she had to compensate for it by being extra good at everything, including fitness.

Melissa had come into nursing late, having been to art school first. She had always dreamed of being an artist and her parents very sensibly let her pursue her ambition, but after a spell at art school she became disillusioned. It was natural for her to progress into the world of medicine, for her father was a professor of neurology at a London teaching hospital and before her marriage her mother had been a nurse. Melissa knew they had both been pleased when she had taken up nursing, although they had gone out of their way not to apply pressure on her to do so. There was only one disadvantage, she often thought, and that was she sometimes felt she didn't fit in with the giggly girls around her. I suppose I'm just too long in the tooth to be giggly, she used to tell herself.

Once back on the ward she reported to Sister, who told her she could go off duty as the evening nurses had already reported for duty.

'I hope you enjoyed your first day with us,' she said as Melissa prepared to leave.

'Yes, thank you, Sister, I did,' replied Melissa. 'It has been an interesting day.'

Later that evening, after Melissa had changed from her uniform and was in her poky little room listening to some music, she reflected that it had indeed been an interesting day. Her thoughts returned to Blake van Reenen more often than she would have wished, but what a compelling sort of man he was. There was an attractive aura around him, she had to admit to that. She idly wondered whether he was as cold and hard-hearted as everyone said; but no, she knew he wasn't hard-hearted, one could see that in his dealings with patients. And somehow, she instinctively felt that there was an underlying passionate side to his nature, which was kept well in check.

She felt very restless that night and when Di rang her on the internal hospital phone and asked her if she would like to come out for a Chinese meal, Melissa accepted with alacrity. She didn't feel like staying in alone that evening, and felt even less like fiddling about in the tiny kitchen she shared with four others, trying to cook herself a meal.

She met Di and another girl, Jane, outside the nurses' home, or the Stalag, as it was nicknamed, and together they walked into the town for their meal. Jane was a staff nurse on the neurological ward, which was directly below the neurosurgical ward where Di and Melissa worked. She had been there three years.

'I sometimes wish I could go on and get promotion somewhere,' she confessed to Melissa. 'But my boyfriend is a senior house officer. He's always a senior house officer,' she lamented. 'First in Casualty, then in medicine and now in obstetrics and gynaecology. I'm just praying that he is going to decide soon which speciality he does want to stay in. Then perhaps he'll ask me to marry him.'

'You're a fool,' said Di. She was a very practical girl. 'You get on with your own career. If he loves you enough he'll ask you to marry him.'

Melissa agreed. 'It sounds as if he needs someone to push him into a decision about marriage and medicine,' she said. 'He can't go on being a senior house officer for ever.'

Jane laughed. 'Yes, I think that fact is at last beginning to dawn on him. He's so much older now than all the other SHOs.'

'Like me and the other nurses,' said Melissa.

'Oh, rubbish,' retorted Di. 'Just because you are twenty-five and most of us are only twenty-two, doesn't make you a grandmother!'

Melissa laughed. 'Thanks for the compliment, Di.'

Jane and Di started gossiping about the Neuro Unit and the staff in it, alighting eventually on the subject of Blake van Reenen. Melissa was interested to know more about him, but she carefully hid her interest behind a shield of indifference. She knew how quickly Di would put two and two together and promptly make five!

'How long has Mr van Reenen been here?' she asked casually. 'It can't have been long because although I trained here I must say that I had never heard of him before I was due to work in the neurosurgical ward.'

'Well,' said Di, 'he's only been here six months. But my word, he has certainly made his mark in those six months! He took over from Sir Frederick Bruce when he retired as senior neurosurgeon, and everyone instantly thought they would have an easy time because Sir Freddy was such a tyrant. But it seems they've picked someone just as bad. And, what's worse, we are stuck with him for years because he is so young.'

'Where did he come from?' asked Melissa. 'Was he a senior registrar in London?'

'Only for a short while,' replied Di, who always knew everything there was to know about everyone. 'He did most of his training in South Africa, where he was born, but then apparently he decided he wanted to practise medicine over here and so emigrated to England.'

'South Africa?' Melissa was surprised. 'But he doesn't have a trace of an accent.'

'Oh, that was because he was educated at some very exclusive school in Switzerland and then went to Cambridge to do his medical degree, before going back to South Africa to start his practical medicine,' said Di.

'Yes,' went on Jane, 'apparently he felt he was more European than South African and that is why he came back here.'

'How on earth do you know all these minute details

about him?' asked Melissa, laughing. 'Is everybody's life an open book to you two?'

'Practically everybody's,' said Di with relish, and she proceeded to launch into the lurid details of Mike Chambers' love life. He was the latest registrar to join the ranks in neurology.

When she left Di and Jane, who lived on the ground floor of the small nurses' block, Melissa went up to her room on the sixth floor feeling strangely lonely. For once she used the lift. It had been a long day and she felt inexplicably depressed.

Once in bed, sleep evaded her. Blake van Reenen's tall, distinguished image, with the sprinkling of silver in his hair and the tiny lines crinkling the edges of his hooded, slatey-cool eyes, came before her. She went over in her mind everything the other girls had told her about him.

She was attracted to him, she knew that. But all I've done, she thought to herself scornfully, is to make him aware of me by being late and then dropping that damned frog! Oh, curse you, Charlie, she thought, turning over and pumping up her pillow viciously in an effort to get more comfortable.

She drifted off eventually into a restless sleep, dreaming that she was in Blake van Reenen's arms and that he was being far from cold-blooded! Waking, she stretched up her arms luxuriously in the dark. What a lovely dream! She smiled to herself. And that, my girl, she thought, is about as near to him as you are ever likely to get—in a dream!

Then she realised what had woken her up. She was terribly thirsty. Wishing she had never eaten all that Chinese food because it always had the same effect on her, she climbed reluctantly out of bed and slipped on her cotton dressing-gown.

There was nothing for it, she would just have to go down the corridor to the kitchen and get herself a glass of milk. That was one of the major disadvantages of living in the nurses' home, having to share everything. And these days the rooms were occupied by both men and women, and some junior doctors as well as nurses. So that meant never being able to slip out to the bathroom or kitchen in just a nightie, never knowing who one might meet in the corridor.

The emergency night lights were on in the hallway outside, giving just enough light to see by. Melissa padded down the corridor to the kitchen and poured herself a glass of milk to take back to her room. As she left the kitchen she heard a door slam at the far end of the hall. Idly she wondered who was getting up and making such a noise at four in the morning. It was practically all girls down that end. Must be one of the female junior doctors, she thought, going off to an emergency. She knew some of them slept in their rooms in the nurses' home when they were on call.

She closed the kitchen door carefully behind her and started back down the corridor, padding silently along on her bare feet, and as she did so she caught sight of a familiar tall figure, a raincoat slung over his shoulder. Her heart did a double somersault. What was Blake van Reenen doing here? And at this time of the morning?

The memory of her dream came flooding back to her. But he had been in someone else's arms, not hers, while she had been dreaming of him. She knew he couldn't have a room in the residence, for he apparently had some marvellous mansion outside town. The only explanation that there could possibly be was that he had been paying a nocturnal visit to either a junior female doctor, or a nurse . . .

He disappeared into the lift without a backward glance and did not see Melissa. She was glad, for she was sure her disappointment was written all over her face. Serves you right, she thought, going back to her room despondently. Of course he didn't notice you, and of course he's not cold-blooded like Di said. Who he chooses to sleep with is his business, not yours! He's a mature man, not some young boy!

All the same, she would never have believed it had anyone told her twenty-four hours before that she would have felt so unhappy at the thought of a man she had only met that day, making love to some unknown woman.

CHAPTER TWO

THE NEXT day Melissa saw Blake van Reenen from a distance. She was with one of the physiotherapists, propping up a patient, trying to get her to walk down the ward, when she saw him at Mrs Betts' bedside. She could see him talking soothingly to Mrs Betts, who was still drowsy from her operation the night before, and at the sight of him her heart lurched unevenly. However, she firmly did not allow one single second of her thoughts to linger on Blake van Reenen or his doings, and concentrated with deadly earnestness on the job in hand. Which was getting large, middle-aged Mrs Timson to put one faltering foot in front of the other.

They proceeded with difficulty and at a snail's pace to the end of the ward and sat Mrs Timson down in a chair for a rest before the journey back.

'Thanks, dears,' she puffed. 'My balance has gone all to pot, you know, since I had that lamin . . . What was it called? I think that's what's done it.'

'Laminectomy,' said Melissa, 'and it's not the laminectomy that's caused your balance to go to pot, it's the fact that you have been in bed for so long.'

'Yes, Mrs Timson,' said the physiotherapist. 'You have been horizontal for too long. Now, do you feel up to the walk back?' This last remark was addressed to Melissa, who was leaning exhaustedly beside the other girl against the wall.

'I'm game, if you are,' said Melissa, gritting her teeth

for the arduous journey back to Mrs Timson's bed.

They were about half-way there when Blake van Reenen passed them.

'Good morning, ladies,' he said. His cool voice sounded slightly amused. 'Don't mow me down in the rush!' His tall, lean figure was past them in an instant as he went down the ward and out through the doors.

'Gorgeous, isn't he?' breathed the physiotherapist. 'I'm always wishing he'd look in my direction. Although he apparently doesn't have much interest in women.'

'All right if you like that sort of thing,' said Melissa shortly. 'Although he is definitely not my type.' Chance would be a fine thing, she thought wryly, struggling with Mrs Timson, who seemed to be leaning lopsidedly, all her weight going on Melissa's side. The sight of him brought back the memory of his tall figure last night, leaving the nurses' home at four in the morning. It also brought back those gnawing fingers of jealousy, wondering who it was he had been spending the night with.

Melissa's wandering thoughts were interrupted by their arrival back at Mrs Timson's bed. At last they were able to deposit their burden. It was difficult to know who, of the three, was the most grateful to arrive back—Mrs Timson or either of the two girls!

The physiotherapist went rushing off; she had another patient waiting for her in the gym. 'Can you manage?' she asked before she left.

'Yes, you go. We'll be all right, won't we, Mrs Timson?' Melissa replied, humping Mrs Timson back into bed.

'Yes, dear. Oh, thank you,' she grunted as she heaved her fourteen stones into position. 'I don't know how you young nurses manage. You're only a slip of a thing.'

Melissa smiled. 'Thank you for the compliment, but according to this diet sheet here on your notes you should now be only a slip of a thing too!' She picked up the diet sheet and looked at it. 'Only eight hundred calories a day. How is it you haven't wasted away, Mrs Timson?'

Mrs Timson wriggled rather guiltily in the bed. 'I always eat what they send me up from the kitchen,' she began.

'Yes, but what else do you eat that they don't send up from the kitchen?' said Melissa sternly and went over to the bedside locker. Inside there were three packets of chocolate biscuits, apples, oranges and some chewy toffees. 'Does Sister know about this?' she asked.

'Oh, don't tell Sister,' whispered Mrs Timson, looking terrified at the thought. 'Let it be our little secret, Nurse.'

Melissa thought for a moment. 'All right then,' she said. 'But only on one condition.'

Mrs Timson nodded eagerly. 'I'll do anything,' she said quickly.

'The condition is that I take this food away and you promise me that you won't accept anything else from your visitors.'

'I promise,' said Mrs Timson, handing Melissa the biscuits and sweets from the bedside locker.

Melissa took them from her, stuffing the two packets of biscuits in her uniform pocket and carrying the rest. It was quite an armful and she had only taken a few steps away from Mrs Timson when suddenly she saw the tall figure of Blake van Reenen bearing down upon her.

'I suppose you thought Mrs Timson needed building up after her operation!' The steely sarcasm of his voice shook Melissa to the core. How could he think her to be so stupid as to give extra food to a patient on a diet! She was about to snap back at him that she was taking the food away from Mrs Timson when she saw the woman's face. Her expression was one of abject pleading, frantically signalling to Melissa not to give her away.

'*Mr* van Reenen,' Melissa heard her voice flashing back at him angrily before she could stop herself, 'I may not be as clever as you, but I am not stupid. This food,' she lied coolly, 'has been given to me by one of the other patient's visitors and I am in the process of taking it to the kitchen.'

She brushed past him angrily, hoping that he would swallow her story about the food so that she wasn't forced to give Mrs Timson away. Anyway, how dare he even think she would give food to a patient on a diet!

Still angry, she opened the cupboard doors in the kitchen and virtually threw in the biscuits and the other food. Damn Mrs Timson, and damn Blake van Reenen! Pompous, conceited prig! Now she knew why he didn't have a wife or seemingly regular girlfriend. He was too insufferable! Nobody would be able to stand his company for any length of time!

When she came out of the kitchen she saw his tall, lean figure bending over Sister's desk and talking to her while he flicked through some notes. It was time for the drug round, so Melissa went to find Lucy. I don't know whether I'm going to be able to stand working on this ward with that man around, she thought rebelliously.

'What's up?' asked Lucy when she joined her. 'You look as black as thunder.'

'Nothing,' muttered Melissa under her breath.

'Oh come on,' persisted Lucy. 'It must be something.'

'All right! If you must know,' burst out Melissa, 'it's that damned Blake van Reenen. Do you know he virtually accused me of giving Mrs Timson extra food?'

'Well, we all know Mrs Timson must have extra food, otherwise she would be losing weight as she ought to be.'

'I know that,' said Melissa angrily. 'But I was taking the food from her locker away, not putting it there!'

'Did you tell him that?' asked Lucy practically.

'No, of course not,' admitted Melissa. 'How could I get poor Mrs Timson into trouble?'

'Poor Mrs Timson indeed,' snorted Lucy. 'All the trouble Mr van Reenen went through to do a difficult laminectomy on her and she hasn't even bothered to try to lose weight to help herself! I haven't got any patience with her at all.'

'Yes, but all the same,' said Melissa angrily, snapping open the lid of the drugs trolley, 'he could have credited me with some common sense. Surely he must know I wouldn't give her any food, other than what she is supposed to have.'

'Sometimes I don't think he credits anyone with any sense at all,' said Lucy, smiling.

'You mean he's got a God complex,' said Melissa abruptly. 'Well, as far as I'm concerned, he is definitely *not* God!' She started pushing the trolley angrily and Lucy had to almost run to keep up with her.

'Steady on,' she said. 'We'll cop it from Sister if we rush around the ward like this.'

'I shall cop it, as you put it, whatever happens,' said Melissa morosely. 'I can't seem to put a foot right on this ward.'

'Rubbish!' said Lucy soothingly. 'You're letting things get on top of you.'

They did the round meticulously. Melissa checked and double-checked everything, until even Lucy complained that perhaps she was being a bit over-cautious! When they passed Sister's desk, Blake van Reenen was still there. Melissa stared stonily ahead, determined not to catch his eye.

'Got rid of the evidence, Nurse?' His deep voice had just a tinge of sardonic amusement to it. Melissa turned and scowled in his direction, but didn't reply. She wasn't going to give him the satisfaction of making her retaliate again.

Sister looked up, puzzled. She saw Melissa's scowl in Blake van Reenen's direction.

'Nurse!' she remonstrated. She wasn't used to junior staff nurses glowering at the senior neurosurgeon in such a haughty manner.

'Oh, it's all right, Sister,' came his voice silkily, which only served to make Melissa even more aggravated. 'It's a private joke.'

Melissa turned her head sharply away and looked straight ahead, her chestnut hair gleaming in the overhead lights of the ward. She pushed the trolley forward rapidly, its rubber wheels moving silently across the highly polished floor.

As soon as they were out of earshot Lucy whispered to her. 'There, I told you that you were letting things get on top of you. He's not annoyed. He knows perfectly well that Mrs Timson had that food hidden there.'

'Huh,' snorted Melissa, giving Lucy a look which precluded any further comment on her part.

Once the drug round was finished, Melissa couldn't wait for the time to come to get off duty. She wasn't usually anxious to leave the hospital, and usually she loved her work, her fault being that, if anything, she was always late in leaving. Always staying on to do other little jobs when she should have been off duty.

What is the matter with me, she thought miserably. Two days' contact with one rather disagreeable man and you have changed. You've met other disagreeable doctors before, she told herself, and you have never let them get you down. Surely you are not going to let one rather young, overbearing neurosurgeon break your spirit?

She thought of her father, Professor O'Brien, and smiled tenderly. She couldn't imagine her patient, gentle father ever treating anyone like that. He would never be sarcastic at other people's expense. He treated everyone with old-fashioned courtesy. It didn't matter to him whether they were the cleaning ladies or doctors, they all got the same kind of treatment from him.

As she went towards Sister's desk, ready to go off duty, Melissa was relieved to see that Blake van Reenen had disappeared. Thank goodness for that, she thought. I don't think I can face seeing him again today!

Once Sister had said they could go, she walked quickly down the stairs with Lucy. They reached the front entrance of the neurological block and wrapped their cloaks tightly around them against the frosty night air, then stepped out through the small pool of bright light that illuminated the entrance foyer, into the darkness of the hospital grounds.

Melissa had said goodnight to Lucy, who lived in another of the residences, and was just disappearing into the darkness towards her own room when she heard Charlie's voice calling her.

'Hey, you gorgeous redhead!' he yelled. Even if she

hadn't recognised his voice she would have known it was
Charlie. He was the only one who could get away with
persistently calling her a redhead!

She turned, smiling. She could do with being cheered
up and Charlie could always be relied on for that. He
came bounding towards her in the semi-darkness, his
white coat flying open behind him, a stethoscope trailing
untidily out of one pocket.

'I'll walk over with you,' he said. 'I assume you're
going over to the Stalag.'

He put his arm tightly round her shoulders and gave
her an affectionate squeeze. Melissa laughed and put her
arm round his waist. Theirs was an easy relationship, not
quite platonic but not terribly romantic either. Melissa
had always been happy to keep it that way. Much as she
liked Charlie, she knew she could never take him
seriously.

'Come on,' said Charlie. 'Let's run. It's absolutely
freezing and I haven't got a jacket on under this white
coat. I forgot it when I came out of theatre and left it in
the locker.' Laughing, they started to run together, their
breath leaving misty vapour trails in the freezing night
air. They arrived at the entrance to the nurses' home
red-faced and out of breath.

'Hope you've got your entrance key,' said Charlie.
'Mine is in my jacket and you know where that is!'

'Now I know why you were so keen to accompany
me,' laughed Melissa. 'You would have had to have got
the warden out of her flat to let you in.'

'How right you are,' said Charlie, hopping up and
down to keep warm in the cold night air. 'You know,
sometimes I think that warden's going off me.'

'I can't say I'm surprised,' replied Melissa, unlocking

the front door of the block. 'The number of times you get that poor woman out to let you in!'

The door swung open automatically as Melissa pressed her key in and they both stepped through into the small entrance hall. Charlie pressed the lift button.

'How about asking me up to your room for a coffee?' he asked while they were waiting for the lift.

'Why?' asked Melissa laughing. 'Have you run out of coffee again?'

'How can you think such a thing,' Charlie answered reproachfully. 'No, apart from the fact that I *have* run out of coffee, I have a proposition to put to you.'

Melissa opened her green eyes wide. 'Really? I can't wait!'

'Neither can I,' said Charlie. 'I haven't had a coffee for at least three hours, and I'm faint through lack of nourishment as well!'

'Oh, Charlie,' laughed Melissa, 'I don't know why I put up with you!'

'Because you find me irresistible,' breathed Charlie and, putting his arm round Melissa, kissed her soundly on the lips.

The lift reached ground level, the doors sliding open silently, and, just as silently, out stepped Blake van Reenen. Startled, Melissa became aware of his tall figure and pulled herself from Charlie's embrace, her cheeks suffusing brilliant red with embarrassment. Why was it that he always turned up at the most awkward moments?

'Don't let me interrupt anything.' His voice seemed cold and disapproving.

'Don't worry, you won't,' Melissa answered flippantly, more than a little piqued at his disapproving tone of voice. What right had he to be disapproving? What she did in her off-duty time was no business of his. No more than what he does is any business of yours, a little voice nagged at her!

Quickly she entered the lift, followed by Charlie, who was completely unperturbed by the encounter with Blake van Reenen.

Melissa pushed the lift button quickly so that the doors would close as rapidly as possible. As they slid noiselessly together she caught a glimpse of Mr van Reenen standing in the small hallway, looking at her with a pensive gaze. After the doors had closed she remained staring with unseeing eyes at the memory of that look. Why did she have this churned-up feeling in the pit of her stomach? Why did she wish so much that he hadn't seen Charlie kissing her?

'Hey, wake up!' Charlie's voice broke into her silent reverie. Melissa gave herself a mental shake and turned her attention back to him. 'Wonder what old van Reenen is doing here?' said Charlie, voicing her unspoken thoughts. 'Perhaps he has a secret affair on the go with someone!'

'What other reason could there be?' said Melissa coldly. 'He doesn't live here, does he?'

'No, I think he's bought some huge house outside town, with about three acres of land. Although I gather nobody has been out there yet—he hasn't had it long. Don't forget, he's only been at the County General for six months.'

'Do we have to talk about Blake van Reenen?' snapped Melissa bad-temperedly. Charlie looked at her in surprise. He had known her for about two years, and in all that time he had never known her disposition to be anything other than sunny.

He squeezed her shoulders. 'No, we won't talk about anything as boring as him, we'll talk about my proposition.'

The lift doors opened and they made their way along to Melissa's room. Charlie followed her into the tiny shared kitchen as she prepared the coffee.

'I fancy a toasted cheese sandwich,' he said, looking at the toaster standing on the side of the kitchen cabinet.

Melissa sighed. 'Get the bread out of the cupboard. This piece of cheese is mine.' She reached into the fridge and brought out a packet with her name on it. 'You're lucky it's still here, it often gets pinched. Here you are, you can make one for me while you're at it.' She threw the cheese at Charlie, who deftly fielded it.

When the coffee and the toasted sandwiches were ready, Melissa loaded it all on to a large tray and carried it through to her tiny bed-sitting room.

'Now, tell me what your proposition is,' she said.

'Well,' began Charlie through a mouthful of sandwich, 'first of all, I know you have got some holiday due to you. Do you think you could take it, or rather ten days of it, in a fortnight's time?'

'Possibly,' said Melissa. 'Of course, I'd have to put in a request to Sister. But why?'

'Because,' replied Charlie, 'I've organised a skiing trip to Livigno in Italy. It's really very cheap if I can get twenty people together. I've asked around and I've already got sixteen. What I want to do is to get a crowd together who I know will all get on with each other.'

Melissa smiled. 'Thanks for the compliment. I take it you think I'll be OK then!'

'You know perfectly well what I mean,' replied Charlie. 'I want people who aren't afraid to let their hair down or have a try at all the ski runs. I happen to know that you are no mean skier.'

Melissa thought. 'Well, it's certainly tempting. I could do with a holiday and the thought of ten days skiing . . .' She paused for a moment. Yes, if she thought she was going to have a break in a fortnight's time perhaps that would help her to put up with Mr Blake van Reenen and his trying ways.

'OK! I'll ask Sister tomorrow,' Melissa agreed. 'You give me the details of cost and so on and we'll take it from there.'

To her surprise, Sister readily agreed when she asked for a holiday. Melissa had been a little apprehensive because it was rather short notice and usually that was difficult to arrange. But Sister had not objected.

'Actually it will be quite convenient as we shall not be taking in quite our usual number of patients over that period. Mr van Reenen is going to a neurological conference in London and then I gather he is going on to friends in St Moritz for a short holiday himself,' she explained. 'Perhaps you'll bump into him on the ski slopes!'

'I think that will be very unlikely,' said Melissa. 'We are going to Livigno, which is some way from St Moritz and hardly in the same category! Apart from anything else, it's in a different country.'

The time before the planned skiing holiday seemed to fly by quickly. Blake van Reenen operated almost continuously the week before he left. Craniotomies, aneurysms, laminectomies, so that there were no urgent cases left. Any other cases presenting while he was away would have to be dealt with by the other neurosurgeon, Mr Wilson, and if he couldn't cope with the workload the cases would be referred to other neurological units.

Melissa had hoped to get up to London to see her parents, but with the planned holiday coming up so soon she had offered to do an extra weekend's duty so that she could have the time off on her holiday without upsetting the other girls' rotas too much. She penned a long letter to her parents, telling them about the work on the neurosurgical ward. She knew her father would be interested as he was a neurologist himself, so she told him about some of the interesting cases she had seen. She studiously avoided mentioning Blake van Reenen's name, however. She just referred vaguely to the two neurosurgeons. It was almost as if she felt that by not mentioning him she could banish him completely from her thoughts. Although, much to her annoyance, thoughts of that enigmatic man had been occupying an increasing amount of time lately.

She had bumped into him several times coming in and out of the nurses' home, and every time had treated him to a frigid stare. He, for his part, had always been painstakingly polite in his greeting and Melissa had the grace to feel more than a little guilty. After all, she told herself sensibly, he *is* a man of the world, and it's none of your business who he is seeing. You are not interested in him as a man, and he is most definitely not interested in you!

All the same, every time she saw him her heart lurched in an uncomfortable way and when he spoke she couldn't explain the prickles that shivered up and down her spine. Her senses were stirred by him to some intangible condition she couldn't place. The reflexes of her subconscious were quickened in an elusive, provocative way. Whenever she was near him she felt as if she was poised on the edge of something totally unknown, unforeseen. It was ridiculous, she knew, and yet the conviction stayed with her.

The last few days leading up to the holiday were frantic. Melissa spent every spare moment either rushing to the bank to get foreign currency or rushing in the opposite direction to organise her ski clothes, skis and boots. She had her own ski suit but it had needed repairing, and she hired the skis and boots from a local shop.

Blake van Reenen had disappeared off to London to the neurological conference. Melissa knew her father would be there and wondered whether he knew Mr van Reenen. Just as well I didn't mention him in my letter, she thought. Dad might have asked him how I was getting on! She could imagine Blake van Reenen's description of her. A scatter-brain who carried rubber frogs about in her uniform pocket and practically ignored him every time she met him! Melissa pushed away a guilty pang at the thought of the cold way she cut him every time she had met him coming in and out of the nurses' home block. Damn you, Blake van Reenen, she thought fiercely. Keep out of my thoughts!

At last the day dawned for the start of the holiday. Charlie had organised everything and Melissa hoped that he hadn't forgotten something vital, but she knew that, in spite of his crazy reputation, when he put his mind to it he could be very methodical.

Twenty assorted people gathered outside the main entrance to the hospital. Charlie had arranged for a coach to take them direct from the hospital to

Heathrow. As practically everybody knew everybody else where was plenty of excited chatter as they stood there in the early-morning darkness, amid a jumbled mass of skis, boots and baggage. The coach duly arrived on time and they were off along the motorway to Heathrow.

Once at the airport it was the usual crush, made even worse by the fact that it seemed that half the population of the United Kingdom were also going on a skiing holiday, all with their skis and a mountain of luggage. Melissa was glad when she finally checked in her own baggage and saw her skis, boots and the rest of her luggage disappear down the automatic conveyor belt. In no time at all their flight number was called and their party went through into the departure lounge.

Some flights had been delayed because of bad weather on the continent, and as a result the departure lounge was unbearably crowded. There was nowhere to sit, it was impossible to get to the bar, and the atmosphere was stifling. Melissa wished she hadn't worn her thick ski suit, although she knew when they got off the plane in Milan, ready for the long coach journey to Livigno, she would need it. She left the others and pushed her way across to the windows of the departure lounge. She knew it was only psychological, but at least she felt that she would be able to breathe a little better if she could see outside.

She stood watching the planes on the tarmac being manoeuvred about, hoping that the flight to Milan wouldn't be delayed.

'Melissa, what a surprise.' It was Blake van Reenen's voice, cool and smoothly self-assured.

Melissa turned and looked into his inscrutable grey

eyes. What was the expression she saw there? She couldn't be sure. He was smiling at her, a devastatingly attractive smile that caused her heart to beat in an alarmingly irregular manner. Hadn't Di said he never smiled! The memory of Di's remarks went fleetingly through Melissa's head, making her hesitate momentarily before she replied.

'You're not going to cut me dead here, I hope,' he said. 'I can't think that I've done anything recently to deserve such treatment.

'I—er, oh hallo,' said Melissa lamely, wishing she didn't feel so hot and stuffy. She was sure her hair, which she had worn down, was in a tangled mess. She hadn't had the energy to battle her way to the ladies' room in order to comb it and she knew that her face must be bright red as she felt so hot.

'Are you all right?' she heard his concerned voice saying. 'You look awfully pale.'

'Pale!' Melissa could hardly believe her ears. 'I feel so hot, as if I'm going to pass out.'

'Yes, that is rather what you look as if you are going to do,' he said. He took hold of her arm. 'Come over here. I can see a seat.' He bundled her through the crowd unceremoniously and sat her down on the empty seat before anyone else got to it.

'Now stay there,' he commanded. 'I'm going to get you a cold drink.'

Melissa opened her mouth to tell him not to bother but he was gone, vanished into the crowd around the bar counter. She sank back on the seat and unbuttoned her ski jacket. She felt better sitting down. A cold drink would be lovely, she thought, but she doubted whether even Mr Blake van Reenen could magic up a drink before it was time for her flight to be called. Her head was still swimming from the stifling heat and she vaguely wondered where Charlie and the others were as she kept her ears open for her flight number.

It wasn't until she saw Blake coming back through the crowd holding two glasses, that she even wondered how on earth he happened to be in Heathrow at the same time as herself.

'Here, drink this slowly. It should make you feel better,' he ordered, thrusting a glass of ice-cold bitter lemon into her hand.

Gratefully Melissa sipped the drink. It slipped down her throat, cool and refreshing. She smiled at him, suddenly shy of this attentive stranger looking at her with such concern in his grey eyes.

'Thank you,' she murmured. 'You don't know how good this tastes.'

'I'm glad to be able to do something you approve of!' The tone of his voice was softly humorous. 'I seem to have an uncanny knack of managing to incur your displeasure.' The piercing scrutiny of his gaze hypnotised her. She felt unable to drag her green eyes from his.

At last she spoke. 'I always thought it was the reverse,' she said. 'I started off badly on my first day on the ward.'

She blushed at the memory. He threw back his head and laughed and Melissa couldn't help thinking how attractive he was. His even white teeth sparkled against the healthy glow of his slightly tanned face, his grey eyes no longer hooded and inscrutable but speckled with laughter.

'It was a refreshingly different start to an otherwise dull day,' he said.

Melissa smiled back uncertainly, all her previous re-
solutions about putting him completely out of her mind
forgotten. Forgotten, too, her earlier opinion of him
being a conceited, pompous prig. She positively basked
in the infectious sound of his laughter.

The spell was broken by Charlie coming through the
crowded departure lounge. 'Melissa, there you are!
Didn't you hear our flight number being called?' He
pushed his way through to them, looking rather fraught.
'I was beginning to think we'd have to board without
you.'

'Oh, sorry!' gasped Melissa. 'I didn't hear the number
being called—and I was listening out for it too.'

Blake van Reenen stood up. 'You can blame me, I'm
afraid, Charlie,' he said. 'I bought Melissa a drink as she
was so hot, and we have been talking.'

Charlie looked astounded. 'Sorry, sir,' he stammered
in surprise. 'I didn't expect to see you here, of all places.'

Blake van Reenen smiled. 'The surprise is mutual.'
He turned to Melissa. 'Have a good holiday. Perhaps we
might bump into each other on the slopes.'

'No chance of that,' said Charlie. 'We're going on a
cheapie to Livigno.' He pulled a face. 'Not the place for
exulted people like consultants!'

For a fleeting moment Melissa thought she saw a look
of envy cross Blake van Reenen's face as she followed
Charlie through the crowd, but it passed as quickly as it
had come, to be replaced by his normal, cautiously
detached, expression.

'Have a good time yourself,' she called back. 'Thanks
again for the drink.'

She saw his mouth move in reply, but his words were
lost in the general commotion. She thought she heard

the word, 'Father,' but couldn't be sure.

The rest of the crowd from the County General were waiting for her impatiently by the entrance to their departure gate. 'Come on!' they shouted as they all bundled towards the waiting plane.

The journey to Livigno was long and tiring. First the plane to Milan, which wasn't too bad in itself; at least there was something to eat and drink and, as it was a daylight flight, it was pleasant to watch the towns and villages below. As they flew over the Alps, the pure virgin snow on the peaks sparkled in the clear sunshine and Melissa wondered where St Moritz was. It must be down there somewhere in that white wonderland, she thought to herself, and wondered what sort of friends Blake van Reenen was going to. They must be very wealthy to live in St Moritz, she reflected.

The more she thought about the brief interlude in the airport lounge, the more unreal it became. As the plane flew forward into the sunshine over the crisp, white, jagged peaks of the Alps, it was as if she was flying away from a dream. From something that had never really happened, something that was only a figment of her imagination. Melissa tried to conjure up Blake's laughing face before her eyes, but obstinately the picture refused to come.

'I'm beginning to wish I'd never asked you,' came Charlie's exasperated voice. 'Do you realise I've been speaking to you for at least five minutes and so far you haven't responded to any form of stimulation!'

Melissa turned apologetically. 'Oh, I'm sorry, Charlie. I was day-dreaming.'

'Well stop it,' said Charlie severely, 'and concentrate on the here and now.'

Melissa smiled wryly—that was better advice than he knew, she thought. 'Yes, Charlie,' she replied dutifully. 'What was it you were trying to tell me?'

'Too late now,' he grumbled, handing her a drink. 'I was asking you what you would like. But now you've got gin and tonic, like it or not!'

Melissa took the miniature bottle of gin with its accompanying bottle of tonic. 'Thank you, Charlie,' she said, leaning forward and pecking him on the cheek. 'This is perfect.'

CHAPTER THREE

FROM MILAN to Livigno was a seven hour coach journey that took them around the shores of Lake Como before starting the climb up into the mountains. When they had been climbing for about three-quarters of an hour the coach stopped at a little village in the mountains for the driver to put chains on the wheels to cope with the increasingly slippery road surface.

Glad of the excuse to stretch their legs, everyone piled off the coach to make for the nearby bar for coffee and snacks. Melissa was glad now that she had on her warm ski jacket. The sun had set and the weather was bitterly cold. It seemed a lifetime ago that she had been sitting with Blake van Reenen in Heathrow airport, wishing she had never worn it!

'The forecast is more snow,' said Charlie gleefully. 'With any luck we'll be snow-bound and won't be able to get back at the end of the holiday.'

'What do you mean, with any luck?' said Tom, one of the housemen with the party. 'That's all right for senior registrars, but I shall have run out of money by then and I shall starve if we are snow-bound!'

'Don't worry,' laughed Melissa. 'You wouldn't be the only one to run out of money.' They stamped their feet for warmth as they walked on the packed frozen snow towards the lights of a small bar on the other side of the village square.

'Funny, bumping into old van Reenen like that at the

airport,' said Charlie. 'Do you know where he was going?'

'Well, not exactly,' replied Melissa. 'I only know what Sister told me, and that was that he was going to stay with friends at St Moritz.'

'Huh, wouldn't you know it!' he snorted. 'St Moritz! One of the most exclusive and expensive places in Europe.'

'Well he is a consultant,' said Melissa defensively. 'When you reach those dizzy heights you will probably be going to places like that.'

'What, on a consultant's salary? You must be joking!' said Charlie scornfully. 'He must have more than his salary to live on. Never does private work, you know. Just isn't interested. He comes from a moneyed family.'

'Really, Charlie,' quipped Melissa jokingly, 'you are as bad as Di when it comes to gossip!'

'Just thought you might be interested, that's all,' said Charlie airily, pushing open the door of the little bar for Melissa.

'Well you're wrong,' she answered, giving him a frosty glare as she walked past him into the bar. What made Charlie think she might be interested in Blake van Reenen? After giving her a curious glance, Charlie followed her to the large, polished wooden table where most of the others from their party had already gathered.

There was a delicious aromatic smell of freshly ground coffee mixed with hot bread and spicy cakes. Melissa sniffed. 'I thought I wasn't hungry,' she said, 'until I came in here.'

It seemed that it had the same effect on everyone and

soon they were all sitting with steaming cups of frothy
coffee sprinkled with grated chocolate and munching
crunchy sugary cakes. It made a welcome break on the
journey before they started ascending once more in the
coach, up the winding zigzag roads of the mountains.

As it turned out, it was just as well they had fortified
themselves with coffee and cakes because, as Charlie
had predicted, it started to snow. At first it was quite
exciting, watching the swirling flakes spinning madly like
a plague of summer moths in the blaze of the headlights.
But gradually the snow became thicker and thicker, and
the windscreen wipers on the coach no longer swished
backwards and forwards in a rythmic motion, but
juddered laboriously, erratically pushing ever-
increasing mounds of snow from the windscreen.

The laughter and chatter on the coach gradually stilled
into silence as everyone realised the difficulty their
driver was having in negotiating the twisting hairpin
bends. All the passengers had their eyes fixed forward,
almost willing the coach to get through the snow storm.
It was with great relief that they eventually came upon a
snow-plough steaming its way up the mountain pass
and spewing out a great plume of snow from the road
and down the side of the mountain. They stayed behind
the snow-plough for the rest of the journey, the narrow
road clearly illuminated now by the great searchlights
on the front of the vehicle. Gradually the coach began
to buzz with the hum of conversation as its occupants
relaxed.

Because their journey had been delayed by the snow
storm it was way past the time for the evening meal when
they eventually reached their hotel. But the manager
and staff were waiting for them, and as soon as everyone

had been allocated their rooms the manager told them to come straight down to dinner as everything was ready for them.

It was a simple meal of pasta, steak and chips, washed down with red and white wine, but it tasted good and soon the long, tiring journey was forgotten as everyone unwound and relaxed.

Charlie stood on a chair and raised his glass to the assembled company. 'To the next ten days,' he said. Everyone raised their glasses in response.

'To the next ten days,' they echoed.

That night Melissa just rolled into bed under the big, fluffy, feather duvet and fell into an exhausted sleep. Briefly, as she drifted off to sleep, the thought of Blake van Reenen flickered across her mind, and this time she saw his laughing face etched in clear detail in her memory. She smiled sleepily as she turned over in her comfortable bed. Don't start liking him too much, came a little warning voice at the back of her subconscious. He's a lot older than you, and is definitely a dark horse where women are concerned. Remember his nocturnal visits to the nurses' home!

The next morning Melissa was awakened by the sound of voices outside and brilliant sunshine filtering through the gaps in the curtains. Leaping out of bed she threw back the curtains and looked out. Already a few keen skiers were coming down the slope outside the hotel. The sun had risen in the clear blue sky over the peak of the mountain opposite, bathing the hotel in glittering sunlight.

Hastily she washed and joined the others for a breakfast of fresh coffee, hot crusty rolls, butter and fruit preserves. It seemed that the next four days absolutely flew by, full of sunshine, snow and laughter. The mornings were spent on different ski runs and lunch-times were usually enjoyed in a mountain chalet, when they ate hot sausage and bread, washed down with cold beer. Then they skied again in the afternoon until about three-thirty when everyone descended into one of the many cafés in the village.

The next two hours were usually spent drinking hot chocolate sprinkled with brown sugar and cinnamon, and eating huge cream cakes. Melissa didn't dare think about their calorific value as she ate and listened to everyone's skiing stories, all of which grew more outrageously extravagant every day.

They had all joined the local ski school and it was quite a sore point with some of the men that Melissa was in the advanced class, while most of them were either in the beginners or intermediate. The following day it was planned that the advanced class would go up in the ski-lift to a very high peak and spend the day skiing all the way back down to the village. It was quite a dangerous run and only experienced skiers were permitted to go that high.

Out of the whole party from the hospital, Melissa was the only one going. Charlie tried to talk her out of it.

'It will be boring for you, Melissa,' he said. 'You won't have any of us to talk to. Or laugh at!' he added.

Melissa laughed excitedly. 'It will be quite an adventure. I've never been so high before, it's a real challenge.'

'Well, I don't know whether you ought to go,' grumbled Charlie. 'Supposing the weather changes? And I think it will,' he added ominously. 'There's going to be another snowstorm.'

'Honestly, Charlie,' exploded Melissa, 'I shall be with other people, and we will be led by experienced guides.' She put her arm round him and teasingly pulled his hair. 'And just because you happened, by accident I may say, to correctly predict the weather *once*, does not make you an infallible weather prophet!'

'Oh, all right.' He made a face at her. 'On your own head be it!'

The next day dawned as usual, bright and sunny without a cloud in the sky. Melissa took a packed lunch that day, for where she was going there would be no mountain chalets or restaurants selling beer and snacks. She joined her party and they set off in the tiny chair lift which was to take them to the top of the mountain.

The skiers were divided into pairs, and as each gondola climbed upwards everything was silent save for the hum of the moving wire and the rythmic grate of the cogs every time they passed a pylon. Looking back down from where they had come, Melissa thought the brightly coloured chairs looked like tiny spiders swinging on gossamer thread up the mountainside.

Soon they reached the very peak, and before they started the descent they skied across the mountain-top in the crisp, virgin snow. There had been a fresh fall and their skis were the first to break the smooth surface.

They skied across to another peak, and, stopping at the top, looked down into another valley. Far away, sparkling in the early morning sunshine, was another town, the spires of its churches and the colours of the buildings clearly visible in the pure mountain air.

'That's St Moritz,' said their guide, pointing in the direction of the town. 'We are actually in Switzerland at this point, and without our passports too,' he laughed.

Melissa stared at the small town across the valley. She hadn't thought of Blake van Reenen once in the last four days. The days had been so full and she had been enjoying herself. Now, suddenly, the sight of St Moritz in the distance brought back the memory of him with painful clarity. His dark lean face with his inscrutable grey eyes flashed before her. She wondered what he was doing, who was he skiing with? She could just imagine his tall, muscular figure skimming down the ski slopes. Somehow she couldn't believe that he could possibly be anything other than an excellent skier.

With one last, lingering look at St Moritz, she turned her back on the little town and rejoined the others. The disturbing thoughts of Blake van Reenen vanished from her mind as she began the long and arduous trip back down to their own little village of Livigno, for she needed all her concentration.

The skiing was excellent and they made good progress in the fresh snow, leaving the shadows of their tracks standing out behind them in stark relief against the otherwise unbroken whiteness. At lunch-time they stopped on a convenient ledge to eat the packed lunch. But they didn't rest for long.

'I think we should be getting along,' said one of the two guides. 'The weather is changing. I think there will be fresh snow.'

Melissa smiled to herself. There would be no restraining Charlie if his weather prophesy were to come true a second time! She looked around at the sky. Surely the guide couldn't be right? It was still a clear, perfect blue with the sun shining. True, there were a few small dark clouds far away on the horizon, but surely they were too distant to be of any importance?

Nevertheless, they finished their packed lunch quickly and started skiing down again. Their village was visible now, like a tiny toy far below them. The clouds that Melissa had thought too far away to be of importance crept towards them with frightening speed. Soon the sun disappeared, and with it the temperature dropped dramatically and it became bitterly cold. A wind sprang up and skiing was no longer the pleasureable exercise it had been, but an arduous, hazardous race against time. They had to reach the village before the storm broke.

Melissa knew now why only experienced skiers were allowed on this particular run. It was no place for a novice. She pulled her scarf up over her mouth to keep out the searing cold, gritted her teeth and, ignoring her now aching muscles, concentrated on keeping up with the others.

The lights of the village loomed nearer, warm and welcoming. It had begun to snow by now, hard, stinging, blinding flakes of snow, but at least they were down among the ski-lifts and on the slopes normally frequented by novice skiers.

It all happened so quickly, that afterwards Melissa was never quite sure what exactly did happen. It was a straight run down to the village and they all gathered speed. Melissa was slightly out to the left of the others and as she sped down the slope, partially blinded by the driving snow, she suddenly saw a dark shape in front of her. Desperately she tried to swerve to avoid it, but the tips of her skis stuck in the thick, fresh snow. She remembered seeing the lights of the village swirling crazily around, and of a stabbing pain in her ankle, then nothing more.

*   *   *

Through a haze she heard Charlie's voice and also that of Blake van Reenen. They seemed to be having an argument with someone else, though the conversation wasn't very coherent to Melissa, partly because she was still concussed and partly because it was half in English and half in Italian. Restlessly, Melissa tried to move. A pain shot through her ankle.

'Melissa, are you all right? Can you hear me?' It was Blake van Reenen's voice.

She opened her eyes and slowly he came into focus. Confused memories of the accident came filtering back.

'Where am I?' she faltered. 'What are you doing here?'

Charlie's face came into view, looking down at her with concern. 'Thank God you're all right,' he said. 'You've had a nasty crack on the head.'

'We don't know whether or not she *is* all right yet, do we?' snapped Blake van Reenen. 'And the sooner we get her away from this place to a proper clinic, the better!'

Melissa struggled to sit up. She appeared to be in a sparsely furnished hospital room of some sort. 'I'm fine,' she said. 'My ankle hurts, and I've got a slight headache, but otherwise I'm OK.'

'Allow me to be the judge of that,' Blake interrupted curtly. 'Excuse me a moment.'

Melissa could see Charlie shrugging his shoulders expressively behind Blake's back as he left the room. She was feeling better now with every moment that passed.

'What on earth is happening?' she asked Charlie. 'How is it Mr Van Reenen is here?'

Charlie sighed. 'Well, after the accident, which by the

way was yesterday, you were concussed. So of course I had to telephone your parents and your father rang Blake van Reenen in St Moritz and he came here immediately in an ambulance to take you to a clinic there. But even he has been having some difficulty in persuading the doctor here to let you go.' He sat on the edge of the bed. 'You were damned lucky not to have broken every bone in your body as well as your head.' He smiled at her. 'You must have had a guardian angel watching over you. All you appear to have suffered is a sprained ankle.'

Melissa shook her head, trying to remember. 'I just recall seeing a dark shape in the snow. What happened?'

'Some idiot abandoned a ski-bike on the slope and that was the dark shape you saw.' He grasped her hand and squeezed it. 'I can tell you, we were all pretty worried when they brought you down on a stretcher.'

Melissa sat up gingerly. She was clothed in a baggy hospital nightdress. 'I must look a fright,' she said. 'You haven't got a comb or hairbrush, have you?'

But before Charlie could reply, Blake van Reenen strode purposefully back into the room. 'That's settled,' he said. His voice had the tone of deep, unquestionable authority. 'You are coming back to St Moritz with me, Melissa, for X-rays and a complete and thorough check-up.'

'But I feel OK now,' protested Melissa. 'Really I do! It isn't necessary for me to go to St Moritz.'

'I think it is.' His tone brooked no objection. 'Besides, I have promised your father that I would look after you.'

'My father?' began Melissa. 'But I don't under-stand . . .'

'Explanations can come later,' he interrupted as he

turned to Charlie. 'Did you bring down Melissa's things from the hotel?'

Charlie nodded.'Yes, everything is here and packed. One of the girls did it for me.'

'Good.' Blake turned back to Melissa and, taking a blanket, wrapped it round her and bent to pick her up. 'Put one arm round my neck and hold tight,' he commanded.

Melissa obeyed meekly, slipping her left arm up and around his neck to rest behind his shapely head where his dark hair grew thickly in small, tight curls.

He swung her up in his arms as easily as if she were a feather and started to carry her out to the waiting ambulance. She savoured the heady smell of his freshly-laundered shirt mingling with the pervasive aroma of his aftershave. For a wild, impulsive moment, she longed to lean her cheek against his hard, chiselled jaw with its faint growth of stubble.

His grey eyes looked down into her wide green ones, his expression as shadowy as ever. 'Ready?' he asked, a curious, almost triumphant smile tugging at the corners of his stern mouth.

'Ready for what?' whispered Melissa, mesmerised by the expression in his eyes. Suddenly her unfettered thoughts ran riot.

I wonder what it would be like to be kissed by him, she thought, looking at the firm curve of his masterful mouth. The mere thought sent delightful prickles of agitation from the pit of her stomach up to her heart. Her breath caught in her throat. Quickly she lowered the thick fringe of her dark lashes, afraid that the look in her eyes might give her thoughts away.

'Ready for the hour-long ride to St Moritz,' he replied

matter of factly as he carried her out into the dark, snowy night, followed by Charlie struggling along with the suitcases.

Once she was snugly tucked in on the stretcher in the ambulance, they set off. Blake sat with Melissa and once he had made sure she was comfortable, immersed himself in a copy of the *British Medical Journal*.

Melissa lay on the couch, warm and drowsy. She felt strangely acquiescent. Perhaps it's the result of the bang on my head, she thought hazily. I ought not to let myself be ordered about by Blake van Reenen. But if he is looking after me, everything will be all right, she thought inconsequentially.

She was still suffering from delayed concussion and her thoughts grew more and more confused. The motion of the ambulance as it sped along the snowy roads lulled her into the transitional twilight world between waking and sleeping.

Her eyelids fluttered sleepily and her long lashes fanned out on her high cheek-bones, pale now because of her accident. As if in a dream, she saw Blake van Reenen look up from his journal. His mouth curved in a tender smile.

'Go to sleep, Melissa,' he said softly and, leaning forward, he brushed some wayward strands of her chestnut hair from her forehead.

Melissa felt herself drifting away on the dark tide of sleep. She tried to speak but no words came. She was vaguely aware of his warm mouth brushing against hers in a gentle kiss. Gently, oh so gently. She smiled in her sleep, happy in the knowledge that now she knew what it felt like to be kissed by him.

The next few days consisted of a series of indistinct

impressions—a warm room, sometimes bright with sunshine, sometimes dark, lit only by a small lamp. People
all in white, soothing voices talking quietly, mostly in
German, and all the time the perpetual reassuring
presence of Blake van Reenen . . .

Melissa slowly opened her eyes. This time everything
was sharply in focus. The room was lit by a small lamp in
front of a mirror. On one side of the lamp was an
arrangement of roses and camellias, their beauty
reflected in the mirror. The window of the room was
large and the curtains were not drawn, so that from her
bed Melissa could see the lights of the town twinkling in
the darkness.

She was alone. She lay there silently, trying to piece
together the confused jigsaw of recollections of the past
few days.

The door opened quietly and a nurse came into the
room.

'Nurse,' whispered Melissa, 'I'm awake.'

'Oh, my dear,' said the nurse in a delighted voice with
a heavy foreign accent. 'I am so pleased. I will get Dr
Bauer at once.'

In no time at all Dr Bauer made his appearance and
proceeded to check Melissa over. At last he sat back,
satisfied.

'I am pleased to tell you, young lady, that you have
made a good recovery. It will be difficult for you to walk
because of your ankle, but even that should be perfectly
fine in about a week or ten days.'

Melissa sat up and stretched luxuriously. 'I feel as if
I've been asleep for weeks.'

'Three days, on and off, to be exact,' said Dr Bauer.

'We were a little worried about that bump you had on the head. At least, Mr van Reenen was more worried than I was.' He stood up. 'That reminds me, I promised to telephone him the moment you regained full consciousness.' He looked at his watch. 'It is rather late, past ten o'clock, but I think I will telephone him anyway. He is living not far from this clinic.'

He patted Melissa kindly on the shoulder and called the nurse over to her. 'See if you can tempt Miss O'Brien with something to eat and drink,' he said as he left the room.

Soon Melissa was washed and freshened up, with a clean nightdress on. She insisted on wearing her own, a pretty blue one, which was much more comfortable than the stiffly starched cotton ones of the clinic. The nurse brushed her luxuriant chestnut hair till it cascaded down in a gleaming mass of gentle curls on to her shoulders.

To her surprise she found she was ravenous and tucked into a meal of soup and cold meat and salad with relish, washing it down with refreshing draughts of ice-cold apple juice.

She found out from the nurse that she was in the St Bernardino Clinic, perched on the mountainside overlooking St Moritz. It was the lights of St Moritz that she could see twinkling in the darkness from her window.

'Mr van Reenen and your father have been keeping in constant touch,' the nurse informed her. She smiled at Melissa. 'What a lucky girl to have such a handsome man as a friend.' Her voice had a questioning tone, inviting Melissa's confidence.

Melissa was not to be drawn. Not that she could have satisfied the nurse's evident curiosity about the relationship between Blake van Reenen and herself.

There were a lot of unexplained questions she would have liked to know the answers to herself!

Although it was late and Melissa had been half hoping that she would not have to face him until the next day, Blake arrived just as she had finished her supper. Slowly he walked round her bed, his grey eyes making a careful appraisal of her.

Melissa was suddenly conscious of the briefness and near transparency of her nightdress. From the expression in Blake's eyes as they lingered just for a brief moment on the curve of her breasts, she knew he had missed nothing in her appearance.

Self-consciously she pulled the sheets up and slid down in the bed, her cheeks staining a delicate pink.

Blake sat on the edge of the bed. 'May I?' he asked, having already settled himself.

Melissa nodded, dumbstruck with shyness as the memory of that warm, gentle kiss he had placed full on her mouth when she was in the ambulance, suddenly returned to her.

'Tomorrow morning I will take you to my friends' house,' he said. 'You are well enough to move now, and then we must make arrangements for getting you back to England.' His look and tone of voice gave no indication that he had any recollection of that kiss. Melissa began to wonder whether perhaps, in her confused state, she had imagined it.

She found her tongue at last. 'Before you start making all the arrangements for me,' she said firmly, 'there are some questions I'd like answered.'

He leaned back and folded his arms. 'Fire away,' he said, fixing her with a quizzical stare.

'Well, the first thing I'd like to know,' she said slowly,

determined not to be unnerved by his gaze, 'is how you and my father seem to know each other so well.'

He laughed, and once again she was struck by the attractiveness of his deep-throated chuckle and the compelling power of his face.

'That's easily explained,' he said. 'Your father has been my mentor since my earliest days in medicine. It was through his influence that I eventually specialised in neurosurgery. So you can imagine my surprise when I found out that the redheaded nurse—'

'Chestnut,' interrupted Melissa involuntarily, without stopping to think.

'Chestnut-haired nurse,' he conceded with a mocking, deferential nod of his head, 'on my ward was one of my best friend's daughters.' He shook his head in seeming surprise. 'I can't think how it is that I've never met you before.'

'Oh, I haven't lived at home for some time,' Melissa told him. 'I travelled round Europe and then went to art school before taking up nursing.'

He smiled. 'Anyway, now you know why your father rang me when you had your accident. He knew I was quite near to where you were, and you know what medics are like, they never trust doctors in other countries. He wanted to make sure his daughter got the best treatment.'

'It was very kind of you,' said Melissa. 'I shall telephone my father and mother first thing in the morning and set their minds at rest, now that I have fully recovered.'

Blake van Reenen eased his tall, muscular frame up from the bed. 'I'll leave you in peace now,' he said. 'I'll collect you tomorrow morning.'

'But that's not necessary,' protested Melissa. 'I'm OK now, so I shall return to Livigno to rejoin the others. I have my return flight booked with Charlie's party.'

'I've cancelled that,' said Blake firmly. 'You will return to England with me on a flight from Zurich.'

Melissa forgot about her flimsy nightdress and sat bolt upright in bed, indignantly. 'You had no right to do that,' she said crossly. 'I may have had a bump on the head, but I'm not a child, and I'm not your patient either.'

She glared at him across the room. He could be domineering to his patients if he liked, but she was not prepared to have her life organised for her by Blake van Reenen, even if he was her father's friend.

He smiled a slow, enigmatic, sensuous smile that Melissa would not have believed possible if she had not been the subject of his scrutiny! She caught a glimpse of a smouldering passion lurking deep in the dark recesses of his grey eyes. Then it was gone as he veiled them with a bland gaze once more and said, in a voice totally devoid of expression,

'Your nightdress has slipped a little!'

Melissa looked down and gasped. One strap had slipped off her shoulder exposing most of her left breast. Her satin-smooth skin gleamed in the dim light of the room. Flushing hotly with embarrassment, she shot down under the bedclothes, thankful that the main light of the room was not switched on. She knew her face must be brilliant red.

'Get out,' snapped Melissa, pulling the sheets up even higher and tucking them in around her ears.

He raised his eyebrows mockingly. 'Your modesty does you credit! But remember, in my profession I see plenty of naked women. One more or less doesn't make any difference!'

His low laugh echoed infuriatingly in Melissa's ears as he closed the door behind him. If she could have got her hands on something to throw at him she would have done so, but luckily there was nothing available.

After he'd gone she lay in bed watching the twinkling lights of St Moritz. Damn the man, he'd left her emotions in a state of turmoil again. The more she saw of him the more she knew that he was anything but cold. I wonder what he is like as a lover, she thought, letting her imagination run riot at the thought of his long, strong fingers caressing her body.

Stop it, she told herself fiercely, he's not for you. You don't want to be another secret affair like the poor girl in the nurses' home at the hospital. Puzzling over his mysterious assignations in the residence block, and wondering who the woman involved was, she fell at last into a restless sleep. But even then Blake van Reenen intruded upon her in her dreams.

CHAPTER FOUR

NEXT morning Melissa rose early to telephone her parents. She felt a little shaky, and her ankle was too painful to bear her weight, but otherwise she felt surprisingly well.

She found some of her clothes in a cupboard but she wondered where the rest of her things were. Probably stored away somewhere by Blake van Reenen, she thought. Anyway, there were some suitable garments in the cupboard and she chose a comfortable pair of blue cords and a large matching blue sloppy sweater. She tied her hair back with a scarf into a pony-tail.

The nurse, coming into her room with her breakfast tray of coffee and crisp croissants, was surprised to see Melissa up and dressed. 'I don't know whether Dr Bauer and Mr van Reenen will permit,' she demurred.

'*I* permit,' said Melissa firmly, and hopped over and sat herself in the chair by the window. 'I'll have my breakfast here by the window, and then please may I make a telephone call to England, to my parents?'

The nurse brought a small table across to where Melissa was sitting and placed the breakfast tray on it.

'Yes, of course,' she replied. 'Mr van Reenen said you would need the telephone this morning. I will bring up a telephone and plug it in the room here so that you can make your call.' She smiled at Melissa kindly. 'I hope you enjoy your breakfast.'

After she had left, Melissa sank her teeth into the

buttered croissant. It was delicious. The coffee was good, too. In spite of the butterflies in her tummy at the thought of meeting Blake van Reenen again, Melissa nevertheless managed to thoroughly enjoy her breakfast. Anyway, it's ridiculous, she told herself, to get so nervous about seeing him again. You are going to have to spend several days in his company, so you had better control those nerves!

As she was eating her breakfast she looked from her window down into the busy streets of St Moritz. The lights were coming on one by one in the windows of the fashionable boutiques as they opened their doors for the day's business. Beyond the houses she could see a skating rink with some early-morning skaters tracing intricate, flowing patterns on the smooth, glistening surface of the ice.

The nurse came back with a stylish white telephone and plugged it in for her. As she thanked her, Melissa reflected wryly that even the phone perfectly matched the opulence of the private clinic. From what little she had seen so far, no expense was spared in the St Bernardino Clinic—from the magnificently appointed room she was occupying to the immaculately clad doctor and nurse. Thank goodness I took out a good medical insurance, she thought. Otherwise all this would have cost a fortune!

She dialled her parents' number in England and her mother answered the phone. Melissa soon set her mind at rest.

'I'm absolutely fine now, Mum,' she reassured her. 'I'm leaving the clinic today.'

'Promise me you'll do as the doctor and Mr Van Reenen says,' her mother insisted.

Melissa laughed. 'I promise. Really, Mum, I'm twenty-five—nearly twenty-six, you know! Give me credit for some sense.' But she knew that in her mother's eyes she would always be a little girl.

Her father came on the line next, and he told her how Blake van Reenen had kept him fully informed of her progress during the three days since the accident.

'You are very lucky he happened to be so near at hand,' said her father. 'I'm glad you are coming back to England with him.'

'Yes, but,' interrupted Melissa, 'that wasn't necessary. I already have an air-ticket from Milan to Heathrow.'

'The journey from St Moritz to Zurich is shorter.' Melissa knew from the tone of her father's voice that he had made the arrangements with Blake van Reenen and that there was no changing them. Between her determined father and the equally determined Blake it seemed she didn't have any say in the matter at all!

'Oh, all right,' she agreed reluctantly. 'It's just that it seems such an extra unnecessary expense.'

'Let me worry about that,' came her father's firm reply.

Later, as Melissa waited somewhat apprehensively for Blake's arrival, she wondered what his friends were like. Would they mind her staying? Although if she had her way, it would be for as short a time as possible.

She applied a little judicious make-up and brushed her hair again. It wasn't for Blake van Reenen's benefit, she told herself. After all, she didn't care what opinion he had of her!

Eventually he arrived and it seemed to Melissa that

before she had time to draw a breath he had her belongings put in his car and she was taken in a wheelchair to the front door of the clinic.

'I'd better carry you to the car,' he said. 'The snow and ice is very slippery and I don't think you'll be able to manage with crutches.' Without waiting for her reply, he swept her up in his arms.

Melissa's heart pounded wildly as she relished the same pungent aroma of his aftershave as she had before when he had taken her in his arms. The pulse in her throat fluttered unevenly as she timidly slipped an arm round his neck to hold herself steady. His mouth was very close to hers. She looked at his firm, chiselled lips. Had it been her imagination, or had he really kissed her on the night of the accident when they had been alone together in the ambulance?

He carefully lowered her into the large car standing outside. Melissa thought it was a Rolls-Royce, but wasn't quite sure as she didn't get a good look and she was not all that well up on the more exclusive end of the car market! After tucking a rug around her firmly, he shook hands with Dr Bauer, who was standing on the steps, and also with the nurse who had accompanied them to the front entrance. Melissa waved goodbye to them and shouted her thanks from the car window, then Blake eased his long frame into the driving seat and they set off.

Melissa stole a sideways glance at his profile as he negotiated the huge car out of the sweeping curve of the clinic's driveway. His face had the healthy glow of a man who had been spending plenty of time in the strong winter sunshine of the mountains. The formidable thrust of his clean-cut jaw emphasised his indomi-

table character, but the slight curve of his mouth
hinted at the sensuousness which Melissa had previously caught a glimpse of.

He turned towards her, his grey eyes smiling. 'I hope
you won't find it too boring, staying with older folks like
my friends and me,' he said. 'I'm afraid we shan't be able
to match up to the riotous conviviality of Charlie Cook
and his friends.'

The ice was broken. Melissa found herself smiling
back at him easily.

'I don't hanker after riotous conviviality,' she said.
'And to tell you the truth, sometimes I feel a bit of a
geriatric with Charlie's crowd myself.'

He raised his eyebrows mockingly. 'If *you* feel geriatric, where does that leave me?' he asked, quirking the
corners of his mouth humorously.

'Oh, you're not that old,' said Melissa impulsively, the
words tumbling out before she could stop herself.

'You mean there's hope for me yet?' His voice had a
laughing, teasing note to it.

Melissa blushed. 'I didn't mean that I considered you
old. I . . .' she floundered. She was getting into deeper
and deeper water and couldn't think of a way to extricate
herself.

Luckily for her, the attention of both of them was
diverted as they saw a bob-sleigh hurtling down the
Cresta run. They were passing right by the run and
Melissa could see its walls, smooth as glass, gleaming
with a blue sheen in the daylight. As the bob-sleigh went
past them like a rocket, Melissa exclaimed in delight at
the sight.

'Oh, how exciting!' she enthused. 'I'd love to have a
go at that.'

'Women aren't allowed on the run,' Blake replied firmly. 'And even if they were, I wouldn't allow you to go.' Melissa opened her mouth to protest at that piece of male chauvinism but he carried on imperturbably, 'Speaking as your physician, of course!'

Melissa closed her mouth. There was no answer to that. Although she had more than a sneaking suspicion that, speaking as a man, he would be just as positive about what he would or would not allow women to do. He would always be the dominant male, sheltering and protecting his woman, she thought, with a sudden flash of insight.

There wasn't much time for Melissa to reflect on Blake van Reenen's character for in less than five minutes he was swinging the big car into the driveway of an imposing looking house not far from the clinic. More like a miniature castle than a house, thought Melissa in astonishment. Whoever lives here must be very wealthy indeed.

'This is the home of my godparents,' said Blake matter-of-factly, by way of explanation. 'Count and Countess Von Baden.' He pulled the car to a halt in front of the imposing stone steps leading to the door at the front of the house. The steps were flanked by stone griffins. The heavy studded oak door of the house opened and a man and woman emerged. Melissa judged them to be in their late fifties or early sixties, and noted that they had the casual, well-groomed look that goes with unassuming wealth.

Blake came round to Melissa's side of the car and swung her unceremoniously up into his arms once more. Melissa's heart lurched in the perilous way it had the habit of doing every time he came near her, but she did her best to ignore it and maintained an outwardly cool composure.

The Count and Countess led the way through to a large, oak-panelled room. A blazing log fire was roaring away in the huge fireplace and books surrounded the walls. The leather furniture was comfortably elegant and on the table and window sills were beautiful arrangements of white flowers. The room had a comfortable, lived-in atmosphere.

Blake put Melissa down carefully on the large chesterfield close to the fire.

'You can stay there for a while,' he said. 'Keep your feet up—that will help your ankle.'

'Yes, Doctor,' Melissa couldn't help replying, tongue in cheek.

The Countess laughed and came forward, extending her hand to Melissa. 'I'm Elizabeth,' she said. Her English had a delightful, slightly foreign accent. 'And you are obviously Melissa. You are just as beautiful as Blake told us you were.'

'He said I was beautiful?' Melissa asked in amazement. 'In spite of my red hair?'

'Titian,' said the Countess firmly. 'Don't ever let anyone tell you it's red—it's Titian.'

Melissa smiled. 'I always say chestnut,' she admitted. She was wondering as she spoke what else Blake had told them about her.

'Of course,' the Countess continued, 'when Blake asked if you could stay here for a few days, we were very happy. We have been like parents to Blake, and your father has helped him so much in his career. It is a pleasure to have Professor O'Brien's daughter here. In fact I'm delighted to meet you at last; your father has often spoken of you.'

'You know my father?' Melissa asked in stunned surprise.

'Of course,' replied the Countess, 'and your mother too! She was very kind to Blake when he was studying so hard for his post-graduate examinations.' She looked at Melissa quizzically. 'I cannot understand why it is I have never met you—but now, at last, we meet.'

'Yes,' agreed Melissa. She understood now, of course. Blake and the Von Badens had felt duty-bound to help when her father had asked. What else could they have done? And, of course, in his usual efficient way, Blake had completely organised everything and left nothing to chance.

'It is very kind of you,' she began. 'I hope I will not intrude on your hospitality for too long.'

'I shall enjoy having young people in the house again,' confided the Countess Elizabeth. 'My daughter, Sonia, comes home today. She will fly back to England with you and Blake.' She laughed excitedly as she spoke. 'She is starting work in London as a television presenter and she will be working in your area, so I do hope you will be able to see something of her in England.'

'Yes, of course,' answered Melissa. 'If she needs any help I shall be delighted to lend a hand.' Although, she thought to herself, that coming from a family background such as this one, and being a television presenter into the bargain, Sonia was probably a very sophisticated young woman of the world!

The Count, whose name was Edward, came back with Blake and they all sat around the fireplace drinking coffee and chatting. Melissa found it easy to relax, for Edward and Elizabeth were charming and easy-going and obviously adored Blake. He might well have been their son, Melissa thought, watching them.

Blake, too, was more relaxed than Melissa had ever seen him, laughing and joking over his coffee. Gone was the coldly efficient air for which he was renowned at the hospital. Melissa smiled wryly to herself. This would give them something to gossip about in the canteen, she thought. What would Di make of all this! Anyway, the news that she had been whipped by Blake van Reenen to a private clinic and was returning with him to England would be hot gossip all around the hospital long before she arrived back. Melissa knew she would have to prepare herself for some close questioning and teasing.

The sound of Elizabeth's voice speaking to her jerked Melissa from her thoughts of the hospital back to the current conversation.

'Would you like to go to your room to rest for an hour before lunch?' she was enquiring.

'Yes, that would be nice,' Melissa agreed. She was beginning to feel a little tired. It was, after all, her first day up since her accident.

'I'll carry you up,' said Blake firmly, springing to his feet.

'No you won't,' said Melissa, equally firmly. 'Thank you, but I'm not an invalid. I shall hop. But you can lend your arm to lean on,' she conceded. 'I don't think I shall be able to manage completely on my own.'

Elizabeth laughed. 'I can see you have met your match in Melissa,' she said to Blake. 'I suspect her will is as strong as yours.'

'I wonder?' replied Blake, his cool grey eyes scrutinising Melissa with a quizzical gaze. 'However, I'm not going to put her to the test. I shan't quibble,' he said magnanimously. He held his arm out graciously to her. 'Your wish is my command,' he said with mock formality.

Trying to ignore the thunder of her heart as she leaned on his arm, and keeping her eyes downcast so as to avoid meeting his mocking grin, Melissa hopped laboriously out of the room. They made their way through the hall and up the stairs towards the room that had been prepared for her. It was much harder going than she had envisaged, and although it would have been bliss for Blake to have swept her up in his strong arms and carried her, Melissa was stubbornly determined to make it there on her one good foot.

At last they reached the door of her room, and Melissa heaved a heartfelt sigh of relief as Blake pushed it open. She leaned wearily against the portal. The struggle up the stairs had taken a lot out of her; she was weaker than she had thought.

Without a word, Blake picked her up. Instinctively Melissa slid her arm round his neck. Kicking the door gently shut behind him, he carried her over to the bed.

Melissa found her green eyes drawn irresistibly to his grey eyes. There was a strange, dark light smouldering in their depths that sent tingles of anticipation up and down her spine. She knew he was going to kiss her, but she was unable to look away. She could only gaze hypnotised into his hard, masculine face, noticing his tanned skin, with its faint perfume of his aftershave and his finely etched features, with their unique combination of sensuality and sternness. She could feel his muscled arms holding her tightly, trapping her within a band of steel.

Involuntarily reaching up her other hand, she gently traced the outline of his firm jaw and, as she did so, she heard his sharp intake of breath before his mouth came down on hers.

She didn't struggle from his embrace. She was a willing prisoner. Submissively she parted her lips, giving herself up to the pleasure of his mouth, gently searching, invading hers.

Still kissing her gently, he laid her down among the soft, full pillows of the bed. Then, pausing a moment, he drew his head back and looked at her. Melissa smiled at him hazily. She felt intoxicated. His kiss had transported her to realms of delightful sensations she had not known were possible with just one little kiss.

'Kiss me again,' she whispered softly. She didn't care what he thought; she wanted him to kiss her again so much.

He needed no second bidding. His mouth came down again on hers, brushing her lips gently with a persuasive, subtle ardour. Melissa felt herself responding. She drew his head down to hers, pulling him closer, and parted her lips pliantly. She heard him give a muffled groan as the gentleness of his kiss became hard and firm. His tongue sought out hers with pervading desire and she reciprocated, thrilling in the contact. She clung to him helplessly, losing all sense of time and space, conscious only of the beating of her heart and the all-consuming fire of his passion.

Suddenly he pushed her back among the pillows.

'You are too desirable, Melissa,' he said hoarsely, in a voice she had never heard before. 'I must be careful, or I will betray your father's trust in me.' His breathing was ragged, his breath coming in short rasping gasps, and she knew he had been as aroused as she had by that kiss.

Melissa lay back where he had thrust her. She wanted him to go on kissing her, drawing her with him into that world of sensual delight she had never experienced before, and was longing to explore further. Yet at the same time she was glad he had the strength to pull back, for she was not sure she would have done.

She lowered her thick lashes, masking the confusion raging within her breast. 'It was just a kiss,' she murmured inconsequentially.

He stood up and, after looking at her strangely for a moment, strode out of the room. But as he closed the door, she thought she heard him mutter, 'Was it?'

Exhausted, she lay back among the cushions on the bed, thinking that sleep would be impossible. But she drifted off quickly and in her dreams she was floating ecstatically in Blake van Reenen's arms!

The sound of Elizabeth's voice woke her. 'Lunch is ready, Melissa. I've come up to help you down to the dining-room.'

The memory of Blake's passionate kisses swept through her like a torrent. Just as well Elizabeth is here, not Blake, Melissa thought.

'Come in,' she called to Elizabeth. 'I'll just freshen up in the bathroom and then I'll be ready. I won't keep you a moment.'

Elizabeth came into the room and sat on the bed and chatted while Melissa tidied herself.

'Sonia will be here in time for dinner tonight,' she said. 'She will be so pleased to see Blake. You know, I've always hoped that those two will eventually marry,' she confided. 'I know Sonia would be only too willing— but Blake . . .' She sighed. 'Sometimes I think he is a confirmed bachelor! What do you think?' she asked as

Melissa hopped back into the bedroom from the bathroom.

'Me? Why, I,' stammered Melissa taken aback by this question. 'I'm afraid I don't really know Blake at all well. He is my father's friend, not mine, and he is about ten years older than me,' she finished lamely, unable to think of anything else to say.

Elizabeth laughed. 'Ten years! That is nothing!' Then she added, 'At least, not when you get to my age! Now, are you ready to come down?' she asked, changing the subject, for which Melissa was heartily thankful.

With Elizabeth's help Melissa made her way downstairs and into the beautiful dining-room. Blake and Edward were already waiting by the fireplace, Martinis in their hands.

Melissa snatched a quick glance at Blake, but never by a look or a word did he give any indication that not so long ago he had been kissing her passionately upstairs.

Lunch was delicious, served by a uniformed maid from exquisite silver on to equally exquisite bone china. They started with crudités, followed by carp with sour cream and capers, then Wiener schnitzel and salad. The dessert was Black Forest gateau, liberally laced with kirsch. A different wine was served with every course and as the meal progressed Melissa wondered how the Countess had managed to keep her wonderfully youthful figure if she ate food like this every day.

Almost as if she could read Melissa's thoughts, Elizabeth said, 'You know, Edward insists on having meals like this served every day, so I am forced to go on a fruit juice-only diet for one and a half days every week.'

'You are ridiculous, Elizabeth,' grumbled Blake. 'I'm always telling you I don't approve of such drastic diets.'

'You stick to your neurosurgery, dear,' she said, not in the least worried by his criticism, 'and I'll stick to my diet.'

After lunch Melissa rested again. Blake didn't offer to help her up to her room. Perhaps he was regretting his indiscretion in kissing her, thought Melissa. The idea left her feeling very miserable.

Sonia duly arrived in the early evening in time for dinner, just as Elizabeth had said she would. She was a tall, statuesque blonde, fantastically beautiful—at least, Melissa thought so. Even if Elizabeth hadn't confided to Melissa that Sonia would like to marry Blake, Melissa would soon have guessed. For Sonia obviously adored Blake and was cautiously friendly to Melissa, evidently uncertain of her relationship with him.

Blake for his part was as inscrutable as ever. He was charming and attentive to both girls, but not exclusively to either. Once, in the candlelight glow across the dinner table that night, Melissa looked up and caught him looking at her. His grey eyes held the same smouldering passion they had when he kissed her.

Melissa's heart almost stopped beating, impervious to the social chat ebbing and flowing around her. For those few seconds they might as well have been alone in the dining-room. She felt her heart begin to sing. Whether he said anything or not, she knew at that moment that he wanted her back in his arms as much as she wanted to be there. All thoughts of his unknown girlfriend back at the hospital, or Sonia's designs on him, were forgotten by Melissa for a few fleeting moments.

But it was only a fleeting moment, for the ardent look in his dark eyes was veiled as he turned his handsome head to speak to Sonia, who was sitting beside him.

Melissa was left feeling strangely empty and depressed. She could never hope to know what was going on in that distinguished-looking head of his. Anyway, she told herself sensibly, he is far out of your reach. Look at the people he mixes with. The aristocracy!

After dinner she made the excuse of having a slight headache and retired to bed early. She thought Sonia was pleased to see her go, though she politely tried to persuade her to stay a little longer.

'Shall I help you upstairs?' offered Blake, rising from his seat.

'No,' snapped Melissa more ungraciously than she had intended. But her nerves were raw and she couldn't bear the thought of being too near to him at that moment.

'Elizabeth has brought the crutches for me, I can manage with those.' So saying, she took her leave of them and struggled upstairs to her room.

Sleep didn't come easily. Blake's dark, tanned face haunted her. As did the knowledge that he had at least two other women to call on when he felt like it. The mystery girl in the nurses' home and now Sonia. And me, thought Melissa miserably, acknowledging to herself that he would only have to crook his little finger and she would fling herself into his arms.

Much later that night, Melissa heard his low voice in conversation and Sonia's reply, followed by her tinkling laughter, as they came past her door on their way to their bedrooms. She tormented herself with the thought of him kissing Sonia, and it was not until the early hours of the morning that fitful sleep eventually came to her.

CHAPTER FIVE

AT ANY other time Melissa would have thought herself in heaven to have stayed in such a wonderful house in the fabled ski resort of St Moritz. As it was, she was so busy trying to appear completely non-committal in Blake's presence that the strain prevented her from enjoying herself to the extent she would have done normally.

Elizabeth and Edward Von Baden were perfect hosts and kept Melissa occupied while Blake and Sonia spent most of the daylight hours skiing. Sometimes they came back in at lunch-times but at other times they stayed out skiing for the whole day, taking their lunch at some mountain-top restaurant.

Melissa longed to be out in the snowy sunshine skiing, but of course it was out of the question. Although her ankle was healing very well, she could only just bear weight on it. She began to look forward to her return to England. At least there I shall be able to get away from Blake van Reenen's presence more often, she thought. Then I shall soon forget him and the memory of those kisses. But in her heart she knew that was going to be very difficult, especially if she stayed on the neurosurgical ward, where she couldn't avoid meeting him most days.

On the day before Blake, Sonia and Melissa were due to fly back to England, Elizabeth suggested that she took Melissa out for a sleigh ride, and then they would have tea in a fashionable restaurant in St Moritz. Sonia and

Blake would join them there after they had finished skiing for the day.

Melissa accepted her hostess's kind offer with pleasure. It would get her out in the fresh air and sunshine, and she had never been in a horse-drawn sleigh before.

They set off after an early lunch in order to make the most of the lingering afternoon sunshine. Wrapped up warmly in furs and rugs, Melissa and Elizabeth sat snugly in the double seat at the back of the sleigh while the driver sat on a slightly higher seat in the front, equally warmly wrapped up.

It was a marvellous experience, gliding silently in the sleigh behind the horse, who plodded surefootedly through the snow, the bells on his harness jingling. They took a route away from the bustling activity of St Moritz town centre at first, and up the small mountain paths where there was no traffic. The pine trees dipped their branches, heavily laden with snow, and cast mottled grey and white shadows as the sun slid through the gaps in the trees. All was silent, save for the occasional bark of a dog in the distance and the ever-constant jingling of the bells on the horse's harness.

Later, Elizabeth spoke in German to the driver and he turned down another path, this time leading back towards the bright lights of St Moritz. Dusk was beginning to fall rapidly so he stopped for a moment and lit two lanterns hanging either side of the shafts at the front, and also lit another one at the rear. The lanterns swung in rhythm to the horse's gait, casting yellow patterns that sparkled as the snow crystals reflected the light.

'I feel like something in a fairy tale,' Melissa told Elizabeth. 'It's all so lovely!'

Elizabeth smiled gently. 'I'm glad you are enjoying it, my dear,' she said. 'I've had the feeling that you have been a little sad these last few days.' Then she added with a laugh, 'Of course, you should really have a handsome young man sitting here beside you, but I'm afraid for now you will just have to put up with me!'

'Oh no,' said Melissa quickly, perhaps a shade too quickly, 'I love your company, and I haven't been feeling sad, just frustrated at not being able to get about. I suppose I'm not a very good patient.'

Elizabeth just smiled and said nothing more as the sleigh drove down into the centre of St Moritz. Melissa looked with envy at the gorgeous clothes displayed in all the fashionable boutiques.

'A pity you haven't been able to go shopping while you have been here,' observed the Countess, noting Melissa's longing looks at the shops.

Melissa laughed. 'It's just as well,' she replied. 'I should only have been green with envy. Everything here is far beyond the pocket of a humble English staff nurse!'

'Oh yes,' agreed Elizabeth. 'I can see that would be a problem. Well, there is only one thing for it,' she said decisively. 'You must marry a rich man.'

'When, and if, I marry,' answered Melissa with firm conviction, 'it will be for love, nothing else.'

Elizabeth laughed and, leaning forward, patted Melissa's fur-clad hand. 'Quite right too, my dear. Money is of no use if you are unhappy.'

The sleigh slid smoothly to a halt outside a very smart looking coffee house. 'I do hope you don't mind if Sonia and I leave you and Blake alone for half an hour,' she said. 'Sonia has a dress she must try on. It has been altered ready for her to take to England tomorrow.'

She led the way into the coffee shop. Blake and Sonia were already there, sitting at a small table in a secluded alcove. As they approached, Blake rose in his usual courteous manner.

'Sonia,' said Elizabeth to her daughter, 'I think we should go immediately to see about your dress, just in case there are any further alterations to be done.'

Sonia nodded and rose to join her mother, and together they left the coffee shop. This left Blake and Melissa alone together for the first time since that kiss in her bedroom.

Blake's grey eyes met hers in a steady gaze across the dividing width of the table. It was as if the whole coffee house had become charged with crackling electricity. The memory of his warm, softly persuading mouth on hers swept through her vividly, leaving her emotions in a state of conflicting turbulence. It seemed like an eternity, and yet at the same time the moment stood still, isolated. Melissa felt as if her vibrating raw nerve-ends must surely show.

Blake broke the silence, but his penetrating, unfathomable gaze never wavered.

'Would you like coffee or hot chocolate?' he asked blandly. The mundanity of his question seemed almost laughable to Melissa, and brought her back to reality.

'Hot chocolate, please,' she replied equally blandly, surreptitiously watching his imperious profile as he turned to catch the attention of a waitress.

They sat in silence, waiting for the hot chocolate to arrive. Melissa lowered her silky lashes on to her high, ivory cheek-bones. It was cowardly, she knew, but it was her defence weapon. She was afraid that the vulnerability she felt in his presence was written too plainly in her

eyes for him to see. She felt so unsure . . . Not of her
own feelings—just being near him was enough to tell her
that in those brief passionate kisses snatched in her
room, not only had he invaded her mouth but that he
had invaded her heart as well.

'Melissa.' She heard his voice as if from a great
distance. 'About the other day.' His voice seemed harsh
and strained to her ears. He was embarrassed; that was
it. It was obvious to her now. He was destined to marry
Sonia, who was from a noble family. A little nurse whom
he had kissed in a fit of passion was obviously a discon-
certing encumbrance. Particularly if the girl in question
should read more into the kiss than was really intended.

'What about the other day?' asked Melissa, purposely
making her voice as cold and distant as was humanly
possible and trying to cover the searing hurt inside her.
'Don't worry about it, I have forgotten about it already.'

'You have?' Was it her imagination or did his voice
sound slightly incredulous? He was conceited if he
thought that she would care, thought Melissa proudly.

'Of course,' she replied airily. 'I take it you are
referring to the time you kissed me.' She took a sip of her
hot chocolate, trying not to let him see that she was
trembling. She forced a brittle laugh. 'Really, Blake,
you surely don't expect me to dwell on a mundane thing
like that? I'm not a dewey-eyed sixteen-year-old, you
know! I only bother to pay attention to the things
that interest me. I've no time for the boring things of
life!'

She had gone over the top, she knew it. She could
have pretended it didn't matter without being so cutting.
Immediately the words had come out she had regretted
them, but it was too late. What was said, was said. At

that moment she had wanted to hurt him, because she was feeling so hurt herself.

Blake's face hardened. Out of the corner of her eye she saw the muscles tighten along his jaw-line. 'It seems I made a mistake where you were concerned, Melissa,' he said coldly.

'It seems you did,' she replied sweetly. Damn the man. Obviously all he was concerned about was his dented ego, never mind her shattered heart.

It was just as well that Sonia and Elizabeth returned at that moment, laden with parcels expensively packaged in fancy paper sealed with little bows. The rest of that evening and the flight from Zurich to London passed in a blur of undiluted misery as far as Melissa was concerned, although to all intents and purposes she was a gay, lively companion. Pagliacci has nothing on me, she thought bitterly.

It was with an overwhelming sense of relief that she said goodbye to Sonia and Blake and let herself into her poky, but at that moment familiar and welcoming, little room in the nurses' home.

After unpacking she climbed into bed. It had been quite late by the time she had eventually reached the haven of her room. Too late, she thought thankfully, for Di or any of the others to come visiting. She wanted to be left to herself for a bit. The last thing in the world she wanted to do at that moment was to satisfy their curiosity about her stay with Blake van Reenen in St Moritz.

To her surprise, sleep came easily. She must have been more exhausted than she thought for she slept like a log until her alarm awoke her with its shrill ring at six-thirty a.m.

Although her ankle was still painful and was firmly

strapped up, she was managing to walk quite well by now and the only visible evidence of her accident was a slight limp.

Her luck was in for once and she managed to dive into the shared bathroom first and then hastily snatch a piece of dry toast and a cup of instant coffee. Quite a change from the leisurely breakfasts of croissants and freshly-ground coffee she had grown used to in the elegant house in St Moritz.

After her quick breakfast she donned her crisp uniform, swept her unruly chestnut hair up into her work-aday bun, fastening it firmly with a wooden pin, perched a clean white paper cap on her head and set off across the hospital grounds towards the Neurological Unit.

Once on the ward, Melissa reported directly to Sister, who seemed surprised to see her.

'I understood from Mr van Reenen that you would not be fit for duty for some days,' she said. 'Apparently your ankle is not completely healed.'

'Mr van Reenen?' queried Melissa in surprise.

'Yes, he came in at the crack of dawn of course!' Sister smiled benignly. 'You know Mr van Reenen. He is not one to let the grass grow under his feet.' She looked at Melissa curiously. 'I gather from Charlie Cook that he took you under his wing after your accident?'

'Yes,' said Melissa awkwardly. 'I didn't have a lot of choice actually, my father arranged it all.'

'Your father?' queried sister, evidently becoming more interested.

Melissa sighed. She supposed she would have to tell Sister that her father was Professor O'Brien, the famous professor of neurology. It was a fact that she usually kept to herself. She preferred to make her own way in life and had always felt that perhaps people would think she was using her famous father's name to help her up the ladder. But there was nothing for it. She would have to tell Sister at least, for she could see her eyes were alive with interest.

'My father is a great friend of Mr van Reenen,' began Melissa.

'Yes, but who is your father?' interrupted Sister impatiently, curiosity getting the better of her.

'My father is Professor O'Brien, Professor of Neurology.'

'Not *the* Professor O'Brien?' said Sister in awed tones, which was just what Melissa had not wanted to happen. 'Why didn't I know that?'

'Sister,' said Melissa quickly and firmly, 'it isn't important. My father may be famous, but I'm just an ordinary nurse. There was no reason for you, or anybody else, for that matter,' she added, 'to know.'

'Yes, of course, Nurse,' replied Sister officiously. 'You are quite right.'

'Anyway,' continued Melissa, anxious to get the explanations over and done with, 'my father was naturally worried when he knew I'd had an accident and as Mr van Reenen was staying relatively close by he asked him to arrange for my medical care, which he did.'

She flashed Sister a look, challenging her to ask any more questions.

'However, Mr van Reenen was wrong about my ankle,' she said firmly. 'Apart from a slight limp I am quite well and therefore I am reporting for duty.'

Sister heaved a sigh of relief. 'Well, to tell you the truth, I was wondering how on earth we were going to manage. There was no chance of getting a relief nurse from the pool, and we have four elective admissions today, not to mention the emergencies that are sure to turn up.'

She took a pile of patients' notes and opened the drawer of the Kardex files in her desk. 'We'll do our usual daily briefing on the notes in about ten minutes. Until then, perhaps you can help SEN Warren finish clearing the breakfasts and tidying the beds.'

Melissa joined Warren, who was in a terrible flap as usual. She was a large, well-meaning girl, but somehow she always managed to turn the simplest of tasks into mammoth problems. As Melissa expected, she was behind with the breakfasts and several patients were still sitting patiently on bedpans, waiting to be helped off. Melissa sighed but said nothing. It was ridiculous for her to do the breakfasts and bedpans at the same time, apart from the fact that it was hardly hygienic! But Nurse Warren never seemed to think of obvious things like that.

'You finish off the breakfast trays,' said Melissa, briskly taking charge. 'I'll sort out those on bedpans.'

'Oh, would you?' breathed Nurse Warren gratefully, red in the face and sweating from rushing around. 'I don't know why, but half the patients always seem to want bedpans at breakfast time!'

Melissa laughed. 'Human nature,' she replied as she set to work. In no time at all the patients were sorted out, and soon they were clean and comfortable, having had their breakfasts. They settled down for the morning to their usual routine, some reading, some dozing. With Melissa's help, for once SEN Warren was on time for Sister's morning briefing.

The nurses drew up chairs and sat in a tight circle

around Sister's desk, while she went through each patient's notes and brought her staff up to date on their progress, commented on points to watch out for and drew attention to any changes in a patient's medication.

'I shall put Nurse O'Brien on fairly light duties today,' Sister told the other girls. 'We can't afford to let her ankle get worse as we need her services desperately.'

'You can say that again,' said Nurse Warren when they had been dismissed by Sister. 'Last week was murder, and that was with Mr van Reenen away! Goodness knows what it will be like now he's back!'

'Murder again, I shouldn't wonder,' laughed Melissa.

'I hear Mr van Reenen looked after you,' breathed Nurse Warren. 'I must say I wouldn't mind him looking after *me*. What was he like?'

'Very bossy,' said Melissa firmly. 'I don't think you would enjoy it at all.'

'Well, I think he's dishy,' said Nurse Warren dreamily. 'Even if he is a bit fierce. Although I suppose he would tell me to lose weight!'

'I don't suppose, I *know* he would,' laughed Melissa. 'So how about not having that chocolate biscuit for elevenses?'

'But I get so hungry,' Warren wailed. 'I've got to keep my strength up.'

Melissa despaired. 'You will never lose weight if you don't show a little will power,' she said crossly. She felt cross because it was obviously that Nurse Warren could easily be a very pretty girl, if only she could lose some weight.

'Anyway, if Mr van Reenen would only look at me as a woman, I think I could do anything!' Nurse Warren swept up her permanently straggling hair with an affected gesture of elegance.

Melissa laughed a trifle bitterly. 'Ordinary nurses like you and I don't stand a chance with a man like him. He's in with the aristocracy!'

Leaving Nurse Warren open-mouthed to ponder over that particular titbit of information, Melissa went across to the patient she had to accompany down for an angiogram in neuro X-ray.

The patient was a young man of nineteen years. He had come in the previous day and was very apprehensive.

'I only came to Out patients because I've been getting these headaches,' he told Melissa, 'and before I knew where I was, I'd been admitted for brain surgery.'

'Try not to worry,' said Melissa reassuringly, 'and let's get one thing clear. You have *not* been admitted for brain surgery! You are going down for a special type of X-ray now, so that the doctors can try to pinpoint the cause of your headaches.'

'Do you think I have a tumour, Nurse?' he whispered, eyes wide with fear.

'I don't know,' replied Melissa firmly. 'When the results of your X-rays are ready, the consultant who has admitted you will come and talk to you. So until then try not to let your imagination run riot.' She smiled at him and he smiled rather uncertainly back.

As the porters helped him onto the trolley, ready to go down to X-ray, she unclipped his notes from the end of the bed.

'Oh, I see Mr van Reenen is your consultant,' she said. 'Well, you couldn't be in better hands.'

The boy, whose name was Graham, nodded. 'Yes,

Sister told my mum that, but when he came round to test me he didn't say anything.'

Melissa looked at the notes. There was nothing there in Blake's handwriting.

'I think you must be mistaken,' she said gently. 'You haven't been seen by Mr van Reenen yet, only by the senior house officer who clerked you in.'

Graham opened his eyes wide. 'Clerked me in?' he exclaimed. 'Do you mean all that business of smelling things like peppermint and cloves, and touching the end of my nose and having needles stuck in my big toes?'

Melissa laughed. 'Yes, that's called "clerking in" on a neurological ward. That is merely listing all your various reflexes and making sure they are normal.'

Graham began to look interested. 'Were mine normal?' he asked.

Melissa wagged her finger at him. 'You know I'm not supposed to tell you what is in your notes. But,' she had a quick look, 'I see no harm in telling you that according to this you are disgustingly normal.'

'Thank goodness for that,' he muttered, and relaxed back on his pillow. Melissa went through with him into X-ray and handed his notes to the sister there. The senior radiographer came hurrying out, her face flushed with annoyance.

'You've taken your time, Nurse. We sent for this patient ages ago. Dr Mangold has had to wait, and you know he doesn't like to be kept waiting.' She indicated angrily to the porters to push the patient through to the angio room.

Melissa bit her tongue. Miss Sugden, the senior neuro radiographer, had a terrible reputation for being an absolute dragon, but Melissa also knew that Dr Mangold was a real ogre. Everyone who worked with him quaked in their shoes. He was a rude, bad-tempered, self-opinionated man, who took out his bad temper on Miss Sugden and made her life hell.

Melissa had only come across him in her student days and had thoroughly disliked him. He had the old fashioned God-complex, and Melissa knew that with her quick temper she would never have been able to put up with his rudeness for long. Sooner or later she would have answered back. For this reason she didn't snap back at Miss Sugden, even though she was sorely tempted. She felt sorry for the poor, harassed woman.

After she had handed over her patient she left X-ray and started up the long corridor past neuro theatres back to the stairs that led up to the wards. As she passed the theatre entrance, the double rubber doors swung open and Blake van Reenen came out in theatre greens.

For a brief moment Melissa experienced unexpected panic at the sight of him. She was used, by now, to her heart lurching uncomfortably every time she saw him, but she was unprepared for panic to overwhelm her. It was with difficulty that she stood her ground and wished him a cool, 'Good morning,' instead of fleeing in the opposite direction down the corridor, as her instinct was urging her to do.

Blake hesitated too, obviously surprised to see her.

'I thought you would be off duty for a few more days yet,' he said. 'I was planning to come and see how you were this evening.'

'As you can see, I'm perfectly well,' Melissa answered stiffly. 'Thanks to your good care of me.' She unnecessarily smoothed an imaginary wrinkle out of her skirt. 'So there is no need to worry about me.' She started to continue to walk past him on her way back to the ward.

As she passed him he reached out a hand and grasped her slender wrist in a vice-like grip, pulling her towards him. She was very conscious of his tall, muscled body clad in his starched surgeon's greens and acutely aware, quite ridiculously, it struck her, of the thick black wiry hair she could see curling at the base of his throat. It was revealed by the vee of the theatre shirt and his sheer animal magnetism struck her like a physical force.

'I told your father that I wouldn't let you go back to work until you were one hundred per cent fit,' he said in a low voice.

Melissa couldn't bring herself to meet his eyes, it was too painful. Just being near to him was more than she could bear. Terrified that she would give her feelings away, she wrenched her wrist from his grasp.

'I will tell my father myself that your duties towards me have been discharged to the full and are now at an end.'

She didn't wait for any reaction on his part but almost ran down the corridor in her haste to get away, her eyes blinded by burning tears. She was just thankful she had got away before she had made a complete and utter fool of herself.

A few minutes later, before she went back on to the ward, she paused at the top of the stairs. This is no good, my girl, she told herself fiercely. You are going to see him practically every day. You have got to get your feelings under control. It's no use dissolving into a gibbering mass of jelly every time he comes near. After all, what is he? He's only a man! In a fiercely determined mood she marched back on to the ward.

For the rest of the morning, not that there was much

left of it, she worked with feverish zeal. Whatever Sister asked her to do she did with double speed, until even Sister gently admonished her.

'I know you've just come back from holiday,' she said, 'but you don't have to make up for the time!'

By the time her lunch-break arrived, Melissa's ankle was well and truly throbbing and her limp was much more pronounced as she made her way down to the canteen.

She was on late lunch, which always meant the choice in the canteen was limited, all the best things having gone first. Disconsolately she picked up a tray and wandered along to the hot-plate counter.

'Only lasagna left, love,' said the woman behind the counter. So lasagna it was. The woman plonked down a slab of pasta that had the consistency of ready-mix concrete just beginning to set.

'Chips as well, love?' she enquired.

'No thanks,' said Melissa, thinking that if she ate all the lasagna she'd have difficulty in making her way back upstairs. Taking her tray, she payed at the cash desk and looked around the crowded canteen for some of her friends. She hadn't seen Di all day, so assumed she must be on a different shift, knowing full well that Di wouldn't have missed the opportunity for a gossip if she had been around.

The only person she could see in the crowd was Charlie, seated on the far side of the canteen by the window. Melissa made her way over to him. He was wading through a massive plate of lasagna and chips.

'Double helping,' he said, noticing Melissa eyeing his plateful as she came up. He pushed a chair back for her.

'Honestly, Charlie,' said Melissa, sitting down thankfully, for it was sheer bliss to take the weight off her ankle, 'I don't know how you can manage to eat that lot! It's so stodgy.'

'Good nourishing food, this,' replied Charlie, stabbing a chip. 'Besides,' he added, 'I've run out of provisions so I've got to have all my meals in the canteen until I can get out to do some shopping.'

Melissa laughed. 'So what's new?' she said. 'You are permanently out of provisions.'

She started picking disinterestedly at her own lasagna. 'By the way, I haven't seen you to say thanks for organising everything for me after my accident. I was really sorry to miss out on the rest of the holiday.'

'Don't mention it,' said Charlie. 'Anyway, once old van Reenen arrived I didn't feature much, he just took over.'

Melissa raised her eyebrows expressively. 'Yes, he did rather, didn't he? I shall strangle my father next time I go home.'

Charlie laughed. 'It gave everyone something to gossip about, I can tell you. You're a dark horse, aren't you, not letting on that your father is Professor O'Brien. I shall think twice now before I flirt with you!'

Melissa groaned. 'Oh, Charlie, not you too?' She looked pleadingly at him. 'It's not my fault my father's a prof!'

Charlie laughed. 'You mean I have permission to take my usual liberties?' he joked.

Melissa wrinkled her nose at him. 'Yes, of course you have permission. I shall be offended if you don't.'

Charlie wolfed down the remainder of his lasagna and chips, washed down by a large glass of water. Putting his arm round Melissa's shoulder he gave her a resounding kiss on the cheek. 'I'll pop in and see you tonight then, when . . .'

'May I remind you, Dr Cook, that we are due to start a craniotomy in twenty minutes precisely.' Blake van Reenen's cold voice cut through Charlie's words.

Blake was standing by their table in the canteen, his hands thrust deep in the pockets of his white coat. He towered above them both in a domineering attitude. The cold disapproval in his voice made Melissa's blood freeze in her veins, and yet at the same time she felt helplessly angry. What right had he to sound so disapproving?

His glacier-hard voice continued, 'When I say twenty minutes, Dr Cook, I mean knife to skin—not me waiting while you are still inducing in the anaesthetic room!'

Charlie gulped and looked at his watch. 'Gosh, yes,' he gasped. 'I'd better get going.' He gave Melissa's shoulder a goodbye squeeze. 'See you tonight,' he said, and then was gone.

Blake remained standing by the table. 'I shouldn't make any elaborate plans for going out with Charlie tonight,' he said, his voice coldly formal. 'I have a difficult craniotomy to do and it's likely to last into the evening. That was why I was anxious Charlie should not be late in starting the anaesthetic.'

'We had nothing more exotic than a cup of coffee planned,' replied Melissa equally formally. 'But don't let me keep you,' she added as Blake seemed to hesitate for a moment.

'No, you're quite right, I must be going,' he muttered as he strode away through the crowded canteen.

Melissa sat miserably watching his broad back as he threaded his way through the crowds. It was easy to pick his figure out, for he was taller than most of the men in the room and there was a certain bearing about him. A proud arrogance, thought Melissa as he disappeared from view.

Now she was back in the familiar environment of the hospital the memory of Blake's kisses that first day at St Moritz had faded almost into unreality. A kind of dream, and yet she intuitively knew it was a dreamy unreality that would colour her life for ever.

Wearily she pushed the lasagna away. It was as unpalatable as it looked. Keeping that memory subdued was going to be difficult, she knew, and it seemed that Blake van Reenen wasn't doing much to help. Although why the hell he should choose to play the heavy father-figure she didn't know. Perhaps it was because of her flippant reaction to his kiss. Maybe he thought she should have taken it more seriously! What a nerve he had! He should never have kissed her at all—he should have thought of Sonia.

Damn, damn, damn you, Blake van Reenen, she thought for the umpteenth time. Get out of my life! Picking up her tray, she took it and shoved it viciously on the conveyor belt taking the dirty crockery to the kitchens. A pity I can't get rid of Blake van Reenen as easily as that, she thought, watching her tray disappear.

CHAPTER SIX

THE NEXT few days passed uneventfully for Melissa, at least as far as Blake van Reenen was concerned. She missed Di, who had been transferred temporarily to Intensive Care as there was a shortage of nurses there. The neuro ward was also very busy. They had admitted a full complement of elective cases that Blake had seen in his out patient clinic before he went on holiday.

After their initial X-ray scans and investigations, it seemed to Melissa that an unusually high proportion of them proceeded to surgery. The immediate forty-eight hour post-operative period after neurological surgery was critical and Melissa and the rest of the girls were virtually run off their feet.

Luckily for Melissa, her ankle grew stronger daily so she was able to shoulder her fair share of the burden of work. She saw Blake quite often, but he was always with either his senior house officer or his registrar, and there certainly wasn't time, anyway, for social chat.

Melissa found that she began to be able to see him and speak to him, when it was necessary, without her heart thumping so loudly that she was afraid everyone would hear it. There you are, she told herself with satisfaction. I told you he was just the same as any other man. You will be able to forget him in time!

She did notice, however, that his handsome face seemed drawn and tired and that he had quickly lost the healthy tan he had acquired in Switzerland. She knew he had been spending long hours in the operating theatre because, as well as all the planned cases, there had been a run on emergency admissions.

As Sister had remarked, that was a feature of neuro. They were either run off their feet or they had nothing to do. There never seemed to be a happy medium.

One afternoon there was a slight lull. Melissa was chatting to Graham, the young man she had taken down to X-ray for angiography on her first day back. Nothing had shown up on the X-ray but he had been kept in for further tests.

'How are you feeling today?' asked Melissa.

'To tell you the truth, much better,' he said. 'And the funny thing is, I haven't had any treatment, just tests.'

'Perhaps the rest has done you good,' suggested Melissa.

'I think you have put your finger right on the pulse with that remark,' said a voice in her ear. It was Blake. He had come over and was standing beside Melissa at Graham's bedside. Melissa smiled at Graham and made as if to move away, but Blake reached out a hand and gently placed it on her arm.

Melissa turned and looked at him. The usually proud and inscrutable grey eyes looked tired, his face strangely vulnerable.

'No, stay, Melissa,' he said quietly. 'I've got good news for this young man. It's nice to be able to share it.'

Relinquishing his hold on her arm he sat on the edge of Graham's bed. 'Pass me over his notes, will you?' he asked Melissa. Obediently she did as she was told. He had some other results on photostatted sheets in his hand, and he slipped them inside the folder to join the sheaf of other notes.

'The good news is, young man,' he said, 'that as far as I can see there is nothing wrong with you. I gather from your mother that you have been studying very hard and that you have been worrying.' He stood up. 'My advice to you is to study, by all means, but don't worry and do leave yourself some time for relaxation.'

Graham smiled, his face radiant. 'Then I haven't got a brain tumour?' he asked.

'You must certainly have not,' replied Blake, grinning broadly. 'And now off you go and phone your mother. You can go home as soon as you like.'

Graham didn't need telling twice. He threw on his dressing-gown and slippers and skipped off down to the end of the ward where the phone was.

Blake and Melissa stood side by side, watching him go. 'It's good to be able to give good news for a change,' he said quietly. 'Just lately I only seem to have been able to dish out tragedy.'

Melissa look at him again. He looked so tired. All the operating he had been doing into the small hours of the morning had obviously taken its toll.

'I think perhaps you should take some of your own advice,' she remarked, 'and make a little time for relaxation in your own life.'

His grey eyes hardened. 'I haven't felt much like relaxing lately,' he said, his voice strangely strained. 'And now, to cap it all, I've got to move into my house this weekend.' He sighed. 'I almost wonder if it is worth it.'

'What do mean, move house?' echoed Melissa in surprise. 'I thought you had a house on the outskirts of town?'

'I do,' he answered wearily, 'but I haven't been able to

live in it because it needed complete redecoration as well
as the kitchen and bathrooms modernising.' He pulled a
wry face at her astonished gaze. 'The previous owners
seemed to have a penchant for purple and yellow, which
I couldn't possibly live with.'

Before she could stop herself, Melissa heard herself
saying, 'Well, of course, if there is anything I can do,
don't hesitate to ask. I'm off duty this weekend.'

She could have kicked herself the moment she had
uttered the words. Here she was, having carefully built a
mental wall between herself and Blake van Reenen,
having at last got her feelings for him under some sort of
control by dint of staying out of his way, and now she had
placed herself at his disposal for the weekend!

'Although, of course,' she added hastily, 'I had forgotten Sonia. I expect she'll be helping you move in.' Or
perhaps your secret woman on the side in the nurses'
home, she felt tempted to add.

His next words, however, made her very glad she had
not been so unpleasant as to voice her thoughts.

'I'd be very grateful for your help, Melissa. I've got so
many things stacked up in my little room in the nurses'
home.'

'Your little room in the nurses' home!' echoed
Melissa.

'Yes. Don't keep repeating everything I say, Melissa.
You sound like a parrot!' he replied in a slightly exasperated tone.

'Sorry,' muttered Melissa, but to her relief she could
see he was grinning, albeit in a tired fashion.

'As far as Sonia is concerned,' he continued, 'she is
much too busy at the moment at the TV studios learning
her new job. Besides,' he added with a smile, 'she is not

very well organised at the best of times.'

'I am, I suppose,' said Melissa slightly acidly, supposing Sonia would be invited round for a cosy dinner for two when everything was in order. While she . . .

He broke into her reverie. 'Of course you are well organised. You've been trained as a nurse. Besides, it will help get us back on a friendlier footing, Melissa. I'm sorry that I offended you when I . . .'

He broke off suddenly as his bleeper emitted a series of rapid peeps. Pressing the button on the top, he read out the digital extension number it flashed up.

'That's the theatre. What can have gone wrong down there?' he muttered as he turned to dial on the internal phone. 'I only left them with a single uncomplicated case.'

Melissa heard him speak tersely to whoever it was on the other end of the line. 'I'll speak to you later, tomorrow,' he said to Melissa, slamming the phone down. 'My registrar appears to have got himself into a massive blood loss situation.' He ran with long strides down the ward and disappeared down the stairs towards the theatres two at a time.

Melissa turned her attention back to the ward, the sight of his broad back as he disappeared sharply etched in her mind. Yes, it would be better to get back on to some sort of normal friendly footing she thought, even if he was mistaken in thinking what the reason had been for offending her.

'Can you help Nurse Warren with the teas?' Sister said, interrupting her thoughts. Melissa nodded and went down to join Nurse Warren in the kitchen, her mind still in a state of confusion. She had done Blake an injustice concerning his comings and going in the nurses'

home. It was nothing more mysterious than the fact that
he was actually lodging there! All the same though, she
knew she wasn't mistaken where Sonia was concerned.
She could remember the tender light that had flashed
into his eyes when he had spoken of her. Not that she
could blame him, for besides being extremely beautiful,
Sonia was a charming, elegant girl.

However, if Melissa's thoughts were in a state of
confusion, that was nothing compared with the state of
confusion in the tiny ward kitchen as Nurse Warren tried
to get the trolley ready for the patients' teas! How she
managed to get into such a muddle over such a relatively
simple task was beyond Melissa's comprehension. The
kitchen was full of steam as the urn boiled over, but poor
Nurse Warren hadn't even got around to putting the
tea-bags into the two large teapots, for she was still
vainly trying to sweep up the sugar she had spilled all
over the floor!

'Leave that, for goodness' sake,' said Melissa in an
exasperated tone. Then she added, slightly more gently,
'We'll clear that up when we've finished feeding and
watering the patients. They are all sitting out there with
their tongues hanging out for a cuppa!'

'Oh yes. Oh, I'm sorry,' stammered Nurse Warren,
redder in the face than usual. Her straggly hair was stuck
to her face by the steam in the kitchen. She stood up and
made a dive to put the tea-bags in the pots, nearly
upsetting the entire trolley in the process.

'Oh, I'm terribly sorry!' She flapped around the
kitchen getting more and more flustered.

Melissa held her tongue with difficulty and, taking her
by the arm, gently shoved her outside the kitchen.

'Go into the loo and tidy yourself up,' she said firmly.

'You can't go on the ward looking like the wreck of the Hesperus!'

Nurse Warren backed nervously out of the kitchen clutching her cap, which was askew, her red, perspiring face wearing a worried frown.

'Are you sure you can manage?' she questioned. 'I feel rotten leaving you to do it all.'

Melissa concealed a smile. 'Yes, I can manage,' she said, thinking that in fact it would be so much easier with Nurse Warren out of the way. 'Just don't be too long. We must get the tea to the long-suffering patients soon.'

Once Nurse Warren had left, Melissa flung open the windows to let the steam out, quickly filled the two pots with tea, and two large jugs with hot water, stacked the teacups and saucers on the lower section of the trolley, added the sugar, milk and biscuits and was ready for the round.

Getting a long-handled broom she swept all the spilt sugar into a heap in the corner. That can wait until the cleaners come on at six, she thought. They always came in during the early evening and did a quick clean round, although the major daily cleaning was done every morning.

She pushed the laden trolley into the corridor just as Nurse Warren, looking slightly more respectable, emerged from the loo.

'Oh, thanks, Nurse O'Brien,' she said breathlessly. 'I wish I could be well organised like you.'

Melissa smiled wryly. 'You're the second person to tell me I'm well organised today,' she said. 'I never think of myself as being particularly well-organised.'

'Oh, but you are,' said Nurse Warren as they pushed the tea trolley down the corridor towards the patient area. 'And you always look so cool, so remote almost. Never a hair out of place!'

Melissa laughed. Cool and remote? What rubbish! If only Nurse Warren knew how she felt sometimes. All she said, however, was, 'Now let's get serving this tea. And do try not to slop too much in the saucers!'

Doing the tea round with Nurse Warren was an exhausting experience. She was so anxious to please, but so clumsy. Melissa saw Sister raise her eyebrows and sigh heavily as she raised her head from the paperwork at her desk. Melissa gave her a faint smile. Poor Sister, she thought, I bet she's wishing Nurse Warren will be transferred soon. Then she can be another Sister's headache!

That evening when she was off duty she felt absolutely shattered. Must be the effect of working with Nurse Warren, she thought tiredly. She decided to do herself some beans on toast, have a bath and wash her hair and retire early to bed with a book. That was about all she had energy left for.

She had finished blow-drying her hair and had settled down comfortably on her bed in her dressing-gown with a novel, when there was a knock on her door. Oh damn, thought Melissa irritably. She hadn't seen Di to talk to properly since she had got back, but she just didn't feel in the mood for chatting that evening, and she had a feeling it was sure to be Di.

Padding across the floor in her bare feet, she opened the door. It was not Di; it was Charlie.

'Oh.' He was surprised to see her already in her dressing-gown. 'I stopped by to see if you wanted to come over to the doctors' mess for a drink.'

'Thanks for the invitation,' said Melissa, 'but I was

feeling exhausted, so I decided to have an early night—as you can see.'

'Oh yes, I can see that now.' Charlie fidgetted about in the doorway. 'I was feeling in the need of a spot of sympathetic company—but still, if you're feeling tired . . .' He turned to go.

He was not his usual exuberant self. In fact there was quite a dejected air about him. Melissa felt sorry for him; she knew what it was like to feel really down.

'Well,' she said slowly, 'I suppose I could make us both a coffee if you like.'

'Better than that,' said Charlie quickly, 'I've got a couple of cans of lager down in my room. I'll go and get them and bring them up here.'

Melissa put her book away. 'OK,' she said resignedly. Whatever it was, Charlie evidently desperately wanted to get it off of his chest. 'You go and get the lager and I'll provide the glasses.'

Charlie was back with the chilled lager in double-quick time and sat himself in Melissa's one and only armchair while she got the glasses out of her small cupboard. Pulling back the ring pulls on the cans, she poured out two frothy glasses of lager and handed one to Charlie. Taking hers, she curled up on her bed and took a sip, waiting for Charlie to speak.

For his part he slowly sipped his drink, staring with a brooding gaze across the room, remaining silent. It was quite unlike Charlie.

'Well come on, spit it out,' said Melissa at last. 'Get whatever it is off your chest. The suspense is killing me!'

Charlie sighed. 'I had my first death on the table today,' he said. 'I've been doing anaesthetics for nearly five years now, and I've never lost a patient on the table.'

He looked devastated; it was obvious that it had hit him very hard.

Melissa sat up. Death was, of course, a common occurrence in a hospital, but that didn't stop people getting upset by it, and she knew a death on the operating table was an anaesthetist's nightmare.

'Oh, Charlie,' she whispered sympathetically. 'I'm so sorry. Was it that case Blake van Reenen got called to urgently this afternoon in theatre?'

'Yes,' he said dully, 'but there was nothing he could do. I don't think it was the surgeon's fault either, but I suppose the post mortem will show something.'

Melissa sat on the edge of the bed nearer Charlie, clasping her glass between her hands. 'What exactly happened?' she asked.

Charlie swore softly. 'That's it, we just don't know! The senior neuro registrar, Willy Radcliffe, and I started off with a very small localised tumour. Everything was going fine, the patient's pressure was good. Willy was just removing the last piece of tumour, which had come out remarkably cleanly, when suddenly the blood pressure dropped to almost zero and we were standing almost ankle-deep in blood.'

Charlie shook his head, as if he still couldn't believe it had happened.

'I can't understand it. Willy wasn't anywhere near a major blood vessel. You expect blood loss from the arachnoid membrane, but nothing like that.'

'What did you do?' asked Melissa.

'Well, I pumped in every sort of fluid I could lay my hands on. I used up all the O negative, all the haemaccel, then went on to saline while I was waiting for more O negative to arrive, but I couldn't get the blood pressure up and neither Willy or Blake van Reenen when he arrived could stem the bleeding.'

Charlie leaned back in the chair. Melissa had never seen him look so miserable. 'So that was that. We lost a man of thirty-seven, father of three little kids. And he had been told not to worry, everything was plain sailing, he would soon be back at work!' He gave a scornful laugh. 'The best laid plans of mice and men!'

He turned fiercely to Melissa. 'The trouble is, we all of us, doctors I mean, are too confident in our own ability to put everything right.'

Melissa put her arm round him. 'Come on, it's a tragedy, I know, but keep it in perspective. You aren't guilty of neglecting your patient, and I know Blake van Reenen isn't either. I'm sure he gave the patient a realistic prognosis.'

Charlie managed a weak smile. 'Yes, I know you are right really. It's just that I feel so damned depressed.'

Melissa hugged him, her own tiredness forgotten. 'Listen, have you had anything to eat?' Charlie shook his head. 'Well, all I can offer is a toasted cheese sandwich as usual, but would you like one?'

He smiled. 'That would be great,' he said. Then he added, 'Can I switch on your telly while you do it? There's a football match on.'

A football match was the last thing in the world Melissa wanted to watch, but she nodded. 'Help yourself.'

Putting on her slippers to keep her feet warm, she drew her dressing-gown tightly around her and went out of her room and across to the little kitchen to prepare the sandwiches. Humming tunelessly to herself, she started preparing the bread and switched on the toaster.

'How would the hospital staff survive if there wasn't such a thing as a sandwich-toaster?' A low voice behind her made her spin round, startled.

Blake van Reenen was leaning in the doorway, clad in old jeans and a sweater. It briefly registered with Melissa that she had never seen him so casually dressed before and that, even so, he still managed to look incredibly handsome and distinguished. Something not many men could achieve in jeans and a sweater! Just as she had thought she had her emotions well under control, her heart suddenly lurched in an unnerving manner in her breast, and she was uncomfortably aware that she was clad only in her dressing-gown and slippers.

'Yes, we'd all be absolutely lost without them,' answered Melissa evenly, popping two sandwiches in the toaster. The delicious smell of toasting Cheddar cheese and bread wafted up.

'Makes me realise that I haven't eaten all day,' said Blake.

Melissa looked at him. His face had been half in shadow before but now, as he advanced into the kitchen, she could see the same desolation as she had seen in Charlie's eyes. She suddenly remembered that he had been there too, in the final moments of tragedy in the theatre not so long ago.

Timidly she laid a hand on his arm. 'Would you like a sandwich too?' she asked. 'I'm making these for Charlie and myself. It would be no bother to make one for you.'

'Charlie!' She thought she saw the expression in his grey eyes harden imperceptibly. 'I won't interrupt if you are entertaining Charlie.' He gave a sudden harsh laugh. 'You know the old saying, two's company three's a crowd.'

He moved away from Melissa, brushing aside her tentative hand. 'It's nothing like that,' said Melissa, determined that for once, at least, he shouldn't get the wrong idea. 'Charlie was feeling very depressed because he lost a patient on the table. He hasn't eaten for the same reason I suspect you haven't.'

She turned and looked him squarely in the eyes. 'I would be very pleased if you would join Charlie and me in a cheese sandwich supper and half a glass of lager.' She pulled a face at him. 'It's not exactly cordon bleu, I know, but it's the best I can offer.'

She walked past him out of the kitchen and opened the door of her room. 'Why don't you join Charlie and watch the football on TV?' she said. 'I have completely abandoned my idea of an early night now, so the more the merrier. Or at the very least,' she added sombrely, 'I hope it will cheer you two up.'

Blake gave a tired, grateful smile that made Melissa want to reach out and throw her arms around him. 'That's the best invitation I've had all week,' he said. 'But to make the sandwiches taste better I'll go to my room and bring along a bottle of red wine I've got there.'

By the time Melissa had made a pile of crispy sandwiches, some of them with pickle in for a change, she found Blake and Charlie engrossed in the football match. She had made quite a number of sandwiches as she suspected they were both probably ravenous.

The bottle of wine was open and stood breathing on the top of the bookcase. Charlie was still in the armchair and Blake was stretched out on her bed. He moved his long legs up when she came in, to make room for her on the end of the bed.

They ate the sandwiches and drank the strong red

wine, which was delicious and rather heady, in companionable silence. Melissa leaned against Blake's crooked knees, feeling happier than she had been for a long time.

As if by tacit agreement the tragic death in theatre was not mentioned. Curled up as she was on the end of the bed against Blake's knees, Melissa watched the two men gradually unwind. She smiled to herself. Although they were two such different characters, when it came to medicine they were very similar. Despite Charlie's previous protestations to the contrary that he would never be a Blake van Reenen of this world, Melissa knew that, given a few years to mature, he would be just the same.

Eventually Charlie stretched contentedly. 'I must go,' he said. 'Thanks for letting me watch the match. I feel so much better. Food and good wine does wonders!'

'Especially the wine,' laughed Melissa. 'I think it was rather strong.'

'So it should be,' replied Blake, not moving from the bed, where he was still comfortably established. 'It was a present from Edward Von Baden. He keeps a very exclusive wine cellar.'

Charlie hesitated at the doorway. 'Shall I help wash up?' he asked.

'No, that's OK,' answered Melissa, gathering the glasses and plates together. 'It will take me just a few seconds.'

'OK then,' replied Charlie quickly. Melissa laughed. She knew washing-up was not one of his fortes. His room usually had about a dozen dirty coffee mugs in it!

Charlie leaned forward and kissed her on the cheeks. 'Thanks for the sympathetic shoulder,' he said. He waved a hand at Blake and left to go down the stairs to his own room.

Blake stretched his long arms above his head and then eased his lithe frame from Melissa's bed. Now that Charlie had left them, her previous penetrating awareness of his physical presence returned. He seemed to dominate her small room with his enormous masculine frame. Quickly she took the plates and glasses through to the kitchen and washed them.

Perhaps he will have left by the time I return, she thought, her mind racing in panic. Keep cool, she reminded herself sharply. You've done very well up to now and it's easy to be calm if you concentrate!

When she returned, Blake was still standing in the middle of her room. Melissa left the door open for him to leave. He walked across to the door without saying a word. This is going to be easier than I thought, she reflected with relief and followed him towards the door.

At the doorway he turned and, without a word, pushed the door shut silently. 'I suppose I should say thank you for the sympathetic shoulder, too,' he said softly.

'Well, I . . . er,' Melissa tried to break away but his arms were around her, trapping her. The wine, her tiredness and the animal magnetism emanating from his nearness all combined, robbing of her free will. She felt herself dissolving against his hard body, caught in a tenuous, confusing web of emotions. As his dark head bent towards her she spontaneously raised her face to his, her glistening lips parted pliantly to receive his mouth as it claimed hers.

An exquisite happiness flooded through her. Her pulse was racing double time and she could feel the uneven beat of his heart through her thin dressing-gown. His mouth was gently, sensually demanding as it moved over hers, and Melissa responded with a passion and willingness that almost frightened her. But she was powerless to do anything but respond as his strong, sensitive fingers gently kneaded her body closer to his, kindling fires of new, wild emotions she had never experienced before. She was still clinging helplessly to him when he firmly put her away from him and held her at arm's length.

'I'd better leave,' he said huskily, 'before we both do something we will regret.'

Melissa blushed. What must he think of her? It seemed he only had to kiss her and she became completely abandoned.

Leaning forward he briefly brushed the tip of her nose with his lips. 'Put it down to the strong red wine,' he said mockingly. 'Edward told me it was an aphrodisiac, but I didn't believe him at the time!'

'I'm sorry,' muttered Melissa. 'I don't know what you must think of me.'

Blake laughed gently and shook her by the shoulders. 'I think you are a very attractive girl, and that we have both had a little too much wine, plus the fact that we are tired. Tomorrow,' he said briskly, 'we shall both have forgotten about it and everything will be back to normal. Goodnight Melissa.'

Long after he had gone, Melissa lay on the bed unable to sleep. *She* would never forget it, even if he did.

CHAPTER SEVEN

THE NEXT day when Melissa reported for duty, Sister informed her that they were going to be short-staffed that day. It seemed Nurse Warren had come out in spots and measles was suspected.

'Just like that girl to start a measles epidemic on the ward,' grumbled Sister. 'She has a unique gift for causing trouble wherever she goes!'

Melissa laughed. Poor Nurse Warren—*everything* happened to her. 'Well, you needn't worry about me, Sister,' she assured her. 'I had measles when I was a child.'

'That's something to be thankful for,' replied Sister briskly. 'And anyway, although I don't really like saying it, I have a sneaking feeling things will run a little more smoothly without our ministering angel, Nurse Warren!'

The other girls laughed as they drew up their chairs and settled down for the morning briefing. There was not a lot of updating to do that day as practically the whole ward was post-operative from the previous two days' heavy operating schedules. That left no room for new admissions and unless there were any emergencies there was no operating planned.

'Looks like it might be a quiet weekend, with any luck,' said Lucy. 'I come on again at midday tomorrow and they tell me the great Mr van Reenen is off duty this weekend.' She folded her arms with satisfaction. 'At least Mr Wilson doesn't believe in operating at weekends, only if it is a matter of life or death.'

Sister smiled. 'Oh, I believe we shall be seeing a change of tactics in Mr van Reenen soon,' she said. 'He's moving into his house this weekend, and I gather he is very friendly with that glamorous new TV announcer, Sonia Baden.' She turned to Melissa. 'But of course, I had forgotten. You probably know her.'

Melissa sat silent, feeling quite numb, her heart sinking miserably into her boots. Of course, Sonia. She had completely forgotten about Sonia, still being in a semi-euphoric state as a result of Blake's kiss the previous night.

Sister's voice startled her back to reality. 'Didn't you meet her while you were in Switzerland?'

Quickly Melissa jerked her thoughts back to the present. She looked at Sister and the sea of expectant faces around her waiting for her reply.

'Yes, I know her,' she said quickly. 'I stayed with her parents for a few days after my accident. I think she and Blake . . . Mr van Reenen,' she corrected herself hastily, 'have known each other since their childhood days.'

Sister nodded knowingly. 'I thought there was something in it,' she said. 'She telephoned the hospital twice yesterday and missed Mr van Reenen, but she rang again early this morning and he spoke to her.'

Melissa stood up and pushed her chair back. 'Will that be all Sister?' she asked. She didn't want to sit there listening to Sister gossiping about Blake. It was like a physical pain, hearing his name linked with Sonia's. Although she knew she should expect it. After all, hadn't he said last night that it was the wine, and tomorrow he would have forgotten all about it?

Sister gathered the patients' notes together guiltily and snapped the Kardex drawer shut. She had been gossiping about the senior neurosurgeon with the nurses—not really quite the done thing!

'Yes, thank you, girls, that will be all,' she said.

The nurses dispersed to their various tasks. With so many post-operative patients there was a heavy workload. Blood pressures and temperatures needed to be taken at regular intervals and entered on the patients' charts. All signs of change were to be closely monitored and recorded. The morning flew by and for once Melissa was fortunate enough to get to early lunch.

She sped down the stairs of the neuro unit towards the basement where the canteen was located. As she careered round a bend in the stairs she cannoned into Blake and would have fallen but for his strong arms holding her.

'Hey!' His deep voice sounded amused. 'I didn't hear the fire bell!'

'Oh . . . I,' Melissa stammered, at a loss for words. 'I'm sorry, I didn't see you.' She slipped out of the restraining circle of his arms and he made no attempt to continue holding her.

'I'm not surprised,' he rejoined. 'Your speed was almost supersonic.' His grey eyes crinkled as he laughed.

Melissa laughed back for his smile was infectious.

'I am determined,' she said firmly, 'to get to the canteen while there is still some choice of food left. I can't stand the thought of hospital lasagna again.'

A smile tweaked the edges of his mouth. 'You could always do yourself a toasted cheese sandwich. You do a very good line in those, if I remember rightly.' The tone

of his voice intimated that he was remembering something besides toasted cheese sandwiches.

Melissa felt her cheeks suffuse with heat as she too
remembered what she had vainly been trying to forget
all day—trying to push the memory of that kiss to the
back of her mind, where it could be forgotten. But she
refused to look down this time. Even though she knew
her cheeks were stained pink, her green eyes met his
grey ones with a challenging look, daring him to say
anything further with reference to the previous night.

For a moment she thought he would. Then he said, 'Is
your offer still on to help me move in tomorrow?'

'Why, yes, of course.' Melissa couldn't think of any
good reason why she should say no. Not that, if she was
honest with herself, she really wanted to. The thought of
his telephone conversation with Sonia lurked uneasily in
her mind.

'Unless,' she added, 'as I said before, Sonia can help
you? I wouldn't want to be in the way.' Her voice tailed
off lamely. Was it her imagination or did a puzzled
expression creep into those enigmatic grey eyes?

'Sonia?' he repeated. 'I told you she is much too
involved with all her TV and film people. She won't be
there. I'm afraid it will be just you and me, plus some
workmen who are putting the finishing touches to one of
the bedrooms. And the removal men, of course.'

Melissa edged away, starting to continue on down the
stairs towards the canteen. 'Well, yes—fine then,' she
said.

'Of course,' he said, 'if you are too nervous to spend
the day alone with me . . . !' He didn't finish the sentence. He was throwing down the gauntlet of challenge
and Melissa had no option but to pick it up.

'Nervous of you?' Her voice sounded shrill in her ears. 'What rubbish! Why should I be nervous? After all, you are only a friend of my father's!' With that parting shot she continued on down the stairs. Stealing a quick glance at his face as she went, she could see the barb had gone home. He glowered darkly at her retreating figure.

'You make me feel positively geriatric,' he growled, looking anything but pleased.

'Your words, not mine,' she shouted back gaily, feeling for once she had the upper hand. It was usually she who was discomforted, but this time it was Blake.

'I'll pick you up at eight in the morning,' he shouted down at her.

'OK!' Melissa gave him a jaunty wave as she disappeared round the bend in the staircase. She did feel just a little twinge of guilt at her underhand swipe at him, but quickly suppressed it. Now you know, Blake van Reenen, she thought with no small measure of satisfaction, what it is like to feel flattened. She doubted whether it was a situation he often found himself in.

As she entered the canteen she came level with Di, going in the same direction.

'Melissa!' cried Di. 'It's been simply ages since I've seen you.' They both collected a tray and made their way across to the hot-plate counter.

'I've got so much catching up to do,' Di laughed.

Melissa's heart sank. She hoped Di wasn't going to start probing too deeply where Blake van Reenen was concerned. She knew she was a rotten liar and didn't doubt that it wouldn't take Di long to prize out the fact that she was becoming infatuated with him. *Becoming?* she thought wryly as they joined the queue. You might as well admit to yourself that you are!

She became aware that Di had hardly stopped talking since they had been standing together, and that she had not been listening.

'I feel really mean,' Di was saying. 'I've neglected you and all my other girl friends. But,' she sighed dramatically, 'this is the real thing!'

'What are you talking about, Di?' asked Melissa.

'Haven't you been listening to anything I've said?' demanded Di. 'Well, OK, I'll start again.' Which she proceeded to do with obvious relish. 'You see, on the first day I was transferred to Intensive Care I met this absolutely gorgeous physician, George Shearer. He's a senior registrar, specialises in endocrinology. Well, anyway, it was love at first sight. *Pow*!' exclaimed Di expressively. 'Cottage pie, beans and chips, please,' she said to the woman at the counter, hardly pausing for breath.

Melissa grinned. Love obviously hadn't dampened Di's voracious appetite. 'Just cottage pie for me, please,' she said as her turn came.

Once they had paid, the two girls found a table and Di continued with the saga of George Shearer. If her description was anything to go by, he was a golden-haired Apollo, a veritable Greek god, and the County General was indeed blessed to have him. Not only was he handsome in the extreme, but the endocrinology department of medicine would be absolutely lost without his brilliant diagnoses of all the cases that presented!

It was with some surprise, therefore, that when a tall, lanky, ginger-haired man of about twenty-nine, his hair slightly thinning on top, sat down to join them, he was introduced to Melissa as George Shearer! Di beamed from ear to ear and hung on his every word. He, for his part, looked at Di as if she was the reincarnation of Marilyn Monroe and Aphrodite rolled into one!

He was a pleasant-enough young man, but bore not the slightest resemblance to Di's glowing description of him. However, reflected Melissa a little sadly as they took their leave of her and walked off hand in hand to dispose of their trays, they do say love is blind!

She sat there alone a few moments longer. Di and George had asked her to join them for coffee, but Melissa could see they wanted to be alone for the ten minutes or so they had left of their lunch-break, so she had made an excuse about expecting Charlie to join her.

As she watched their figures merge and disappear into the crowd, a ghost of a smile flitted across her face. She couldn't help wishing a little wistfully that she had someone who cared passionately for her. Someone to talk to at the end of the day, someone to confide in, someone to turn to for comfort. There was no doubt that she knew who she would like that someone to be, but he was from another world far removed from hers. The only thing they had in common, apart from the fact that they both worked at the County General, was her father, and that was a very tenuous link indeed, she reflected morosely.

He obviously found her physically attractive, otherwise he wouldn't have kissed her the way he had. But lots of men find women physically attractive, and that's as far as it ever gets, she reminded herself. Just think of the famous men in history, and all their mistresses! But it was always the lawful wedded wife who stood by their side when anything important happened . . .

She sighed. Much as she knew she wanted to abandon herself to him when he kissed her, she knew she would never do it. She wanted a home, marriage and children. In other words, a stable family relationship like the one she had been brought up in. The fleeting thought of her family gave her memory a guilty jolt. Apart from a brief call when she had first arrived back from St Moritz, and an equally brief letter, she hadn't had a long natter with her mother for ages. I'll phone her tonight, Melissa resolved, and catch up with all the family gossip.

She was just about to pick up her tray and depart when Charlie descended upon her. She was pleased to see he was back to his usual inimitable form, for he had his plate heaped up as usual—cottage pie, chips, baked beans and rissoles!

'Have you got five minutes?' he asked, plonking himself down beside her.

'Yes,' laughed Melissa, 'I've got five minutes.' She looked at the assortment of food on his plate. 'Honestly, Charlie, you deserve to be ill, eating that mixture!'

'Good wholesome food,' replied Charlie, attacking it with gusto. 'Hey, by the way, thanks again for being so understanding last night.'

'Oh, forget it,' said Melissa. 'A friend in need and all that.'

'Yes,' agreed Charlie. He paused, a forkful of rissole half-way to his mouth. 'Funny about old van Reenen though. You know I never would have thought he was the type to get depressed over the death of a patient.'

'Well, he is human after all,' replied Melissa. 'Give him credit for that at least! I know you don't like him.'

'Actually,' said Charlie slowly, 'I've got to know him a little better lately. We've had more than our fair share of high drama in theatre recently, and I must say I quite like the guy.'

Melissa laughed. 'High praise indeed from you, Charlie.'

He turned to her. 'It was a bit awkward the other night. At least, *I* felt a bit awkward,' he confessed. 'I didn't know whether you wanted me to go first or what.'

'Oh, it didn't matter,' said Melissa casually. 'He left almost immediately after you anyway.' She hoped her cheeks were not showing any signs of the tell-tale blush she always had so much difficulty in controlling.

Charlie bolted down the last of his lunch. 'Ready when you are,' he said. 'Must get back to theatre, got an emergency laminectomy to do.'

Melissa raised her eyebrows. 'I didn't know there was a patient on the ward for a laminectomy.'

'There isn't,' Charlie replied. 'This one comes from some district hospital somewhere out in the wilds. They've been sitting on him too long. Only transferred him when his neurological problems became so pronounced that even an idiot could see he needed a laminectomy.' He snorted in disgust. 'Sometimes members of my own profession really make me want to spit!'

Melissa linked her arm through his as they walked towards the used crockery conveyor belt. 'Calm down, Charlie, or you'll be getting high blood pressure if you're not careful.'

Charlie grinned. 'Yes, miss,' he said with mock deference.

They walked out of the canteen together. 'I'm off tomorrow afternoon,' he said. 'Fancy a trip out?'

'Thanks,' answered Melissa. 'I'd love to some other time, but I'm going to be tied up all day tomorrow. I promised to help a friend.'

'OK,' Charlie said easily and without question as they

parted in the corridor, he to go towards the neuro theatres and she to go up the stairs leading back to the ward.

'I'll probably see you sometime next week.'

'Sure to,' replied Melissa, raising her hand in farewell. Thank goodness Charlie hadn't asked any awkward questions about who she was helping tomorrow. She had a sneaky feeling that even his unsophisticated mind might put two and two together and make five! She put the thought of the next day firmly out of her head. She was more apprehensive at the thought of spending the day alone with Blake than she could admit to. Still, he had said there would be workmen there, she consoled herself. Just make sure you don't get too near him when you're alone, she told herself. Otherwise all your good intentions will go flying away on the wind.

Once back on the ward, her worries about the following day evaporated as there was plenty to do. Sister wasn't pleased about the emergency admission.

'We really don't have room,' she grumbled. 'We'll have to put another bed in room six, transfer one of the other patients there, and put the new admission here.' She indicated the bed nearest her desk.

'The other annoying thing is that it is Mr Wilson operating, and he *will* insist on writing up different post-operative drugs to anybody else.' She got up from her desk irritably. 'It does confuse the girls. Come with me, Nurse O'Brien. We shall just have to decide who is the best patient to move to room six,' she called to Melissa.

Melissa followed her, concealing a smile. Sister hated Mr Wilson's drug regime. In her eyes Blake van Reenen could do no wrong and she just couldn't see why Mr

Wilson had to prescribe anything different. It's not the nurses who get confused, thought Melissa irreverently, it's you!

After discussion they decided which patient should be transferred to room six. It was never a popular thing with the patients when they were moved. They had always got used to their own particular little corner of the ward and had usually made friends with their neighbours. They could never understand the reason for the moves.

'It's like musical beds here,' grumbled the patient, an elderly man, 'only without the music.'

'Just shows how much better you are getting,' said Melissa cheerfully, turning a deaf ear to his grumbles. 'The better you get, the further away you can go from Sister's desk.'

'But I like it here,' he persisted.

'You'll like it where you are going,' replied Melissa firmly, 'and now you are able to walk a little you can always visit the others. It will be something for you to do.'

She continued talking briskly and cheerfully as she and an auxiliary pushed his bed. His flowers and cards they had piled on to the bed, his locker would have to be moved later. She had developed a technique of brisk cheerfulness for dealing with grumpy patients, never letting them get a word in edgeways. At least, trying not to. She had found from past experience that this usually worked. By the time the patient had been settled they had usually forgotten their grumbles and were busy talking about something else.

As soon as they had finished moving the patient into room six the bay was cleared and a special bed prepared to take the laminectomy patient.

'I do hope they are not too late in coming up from theatre,' said Sister to Melissa. 'It's very difficult receiving a case with only the night staff on.'

'If they are a little late, I'll stay on for a while,' offered Melissa. 'I've got nothing planned this evening.'

Sister smiled gratefully. 'Would you, dear? That would be a great help. With any luck, perhaps it won't be necessary.'

The patient did, in fact, come up about half an hour before Melissa was due to go off duty. Charlie came up from theatre with the patient because he wanted to put up another drip once his charge was on the ward. Melissa was surprised to see that that patient was a very fit-looking young man.

'Rugby player,' said Charlie, putting in the line for the drip. 'Very nasty lesion according to Mr Wilson, but he should make a complete recovery.'

'I should hope so,' answered Melissa, helping transfer him gently from the trolley to the prepared bed. 'He is so young!'

'If he does make a good recovery, it will be no thanks to his previous medical care,' said Charlie grimly as he finished putting up the drip and started writing in the notes. Once he had finished writing he handed the notes to Melissa.

'There you are, all ship-shape and Bristol fashion,' he quipped as he gave a mock salute and departed, his part done for the time being.

Melissa didn't have to stay on very late—only about twenty minutes, in fact. Once she had made sure the patient was settled comfortably, or at least as comfortably as possible in the circumstances, she called over one of the evening nurses and went through the post-operative regime with her.

'If you need any advice, or if the analgesics don't seem to be working too well, call Charlie Cook. He's the duty anaesthetist tonight and responsible for this patient's pain relief. Look, his bleeper number is here, clipped to the notes. He'll come up and write up something else for pain if necessary.'

The nurse nodded. She was fairly new to neuro and hadn't long been on the evening shift and was looking rather worried.

'It's very important that he gets good pain relief at this stage,' Melissa emphasised,' so if you've any doubts at all, bleep Charlie Cook and tell the night girl to do the same. Charlie is on duty all night tonight. Don't forget, will you?'

'Yes, Nurse O'Brien, thanks for the advice,' she said gratefully. 'Charlie Cook, I'll remember that name.'

Later that evening Melissa rang her parents. After a brief word with her father she settled down for a good gossip with her mother.

'Although I can only afford ten minutes chat,' Melissa told her. 'It's getting near the end of the month and I'm broke as usual!'

Her mother laughed. 'Same old story! But anyway, darling, what have you been doing with yourself?' They chatted on and on. Her mother updated Melissa on her brother's latest doings. He was in medicine too, but at that moment was trekking somewhere in Nepal, working in remote villages. 'Your father doesn't exactly approve,' said her mother. 'He feels he should be getting on with his career in this country. But I approve,' she added firmly. 'I feel sure he is doing a lot of good out there, especially with the children.'

Melissa smiled. Her brother was very determined and a very unconventional character, and she missed him a lot.

The conversation got on to her accident in Livigno and her stay in Switzerland, and from there meandered on naturally to Blake van Reenen.

'He's such a nice young man,' enthused her mother. 'Just the sort of man I should like you to settle down with.'

'Really, Mum! Stop trying your hand at matchmaking,' exploded Melissa. 'Blake van Reenen just isn't my scene at all. Anyway,' she added, 'he's practically engaged to Sonia Von Baden.'

'Oh, what a pity.' Her mother sounded disappointed. 'She's one of the new regional television presenters, isn't she? I've seen her on TV.'

'Yes, so you know how beautiful she is and you can forget any matchmaking ideas for Blake van Reenen and me,' said Melissa, trying to sound as light-hearted as possible. She had been half-inclined to confide to her mother about the way Blake made her feel and how miserable she had been lately, but she was glad at that moment that she had said nothing.

Her mother changed the subject. 'What are you doing tomorrow, darling?' she asked.

Melissa's heart sank. She knew Mrs O'Brien would read all kinds of romantic equations into the situation when she told her. She steeled herself.

'Tomorrow,' she said, 'I'm helping Blake move into his new house.'

'Really, dear?' said her mother teasingly. 'You know, if you play your cards right you *could* end up marrying Blake van Reenen yet! You are not bad-looking yourself, you know,' she added.

'Mother!' said Melissa angrily. 'Get this into your head once and for all. I am not playing my cards right, or any other way for the benefit of Blake van Reenen. I'm not chasing after him. I don't even particularly like him. I'm helping him out from a sense of duty. *Duty*,' she repeated loudly. 'Do you hear me?'

'Yes, dear,' replied her mother soothingly. 'I heard you, and so, I should imagine, did everyone else within a ten-mile radius.'

Melissa sighed. 'Sorry, Mum. I didn't mean to be so touchy. Just don't try to marry me off, that's all.'

'I promise I won't do it again, dear,' said her mother. Melissa was sure she was smiling—she could tell from the tone of her voice. She might as well have told her she was head over heels in love with the damned man! She was pretty sure her mother had guessed, anyway . . .

For the rest of their conversation they stuck to non-controversial subjects, like the lectures her father was preparing for a big congress in Mexico and to which her mother was accompanying him. She asked Melissa's advice on the type of clothes to take, although Melissa knew perfectly well her mother never needed advice where clothes were concerned. She had an inborn instinct for always choosing the right thing. She knew Mrs O'Brien was trying to pour oil on troubled waters!

The allotted ten minutes came to an end. 'I really must go now, Mum,' said Melissa. 'Otherwise my telephone bill will be terrific.'

'All right, darling,' said her mother. 'I'll give you a ring next week.' She didn't mention Blake again, although Melissa knew it was on the tip of her tongue. All she said was, 'Don't work too hard tomorrow!'

'I'll try not to,' said Melissa lightly, putting the telephone down. Tomorrow was Saturday, a whole day with Blake. She felt she ought to have been looking forward to it, but for some irrational reason she was not. Control yourself woman, she chastised herself irritably. You are becoming completely neurotic where that man is concerned!

CHAPTER EIGHT

NEXT morning Melissa set her alarm early. The last thing she wanted was for Blake van Reenen to catch her napping, literally! She showered, washed her hair and blew it dry. Considering she was only helping a friend, and a friend of her father's at that, move into a house, she went to an awful lot of trouble with her appearance!

She carefully selected a pair of fawn cords, then changed her mind. They really were a little impracticable. Suppose there was a lot of dust about—she would end up looking like a chimney sweep! So she swopped those for a dark blue pair. They were very expensive, bought on her last trip to London, and they fitted her to perfection, the immaculate cut showing off her long, slender legs to advantage. It was a sunny day, but as it was only late March there was a distinctly chilly nip in the air despite the sun, so she chose a bulky Italian multi-coloured baggy sweater to go with the trousers. Her hair she swept up in a loose chignon and secured it with a carved wooden pin.

Staring critically at herself in the mirror she made a face at her reflection. 'Not bad—in fact, quite glamorous!' she said out loud. 'Not quite up to Sonia Von Baden's standard, but the best you can do in the circumstances.' The words slipped out involuntarily into the empty room, confirming her previously suppressed thoughts that she was a rival with Sonia for Blake's affections.

'Stupid female,' she said crossly to her reflection, referring to her own wayward emotions, not poor Sonia!

A light knock on the door heralded Blake's arrival. His gaze slid over her in slow appreciation. 'You make me feel guilty,' he said lightly.

'Guilty?' queried Melissa, puzzled.

'Yes,' he laughed, looking her up and down again. 'You look so glamorous that I feel I ought to be taking you out for the day, not asking you to hump my bits and pieces into my house.'

'Oh, these,' Melissa made a deprecating gesture towards her clothes and cheerfully lied through her teeth. 'This is just an old pair of trousers and a sweater I've had for years!'

'You obviously take good care of your things then,' said Blake. 'You'll make someone a good, thrifty wife!'

Melissa looked at him sharply. Did she detect a hint of laughter in his voice? But no, his grey eyes were regarding her with grave solemnity. Locking her room she followed him down to the far end of the corridor where his room was situated. Blake pushed open the unlocked door and ushered her in. The whole place was full of boxes, everything neatly stacked and labelled, ready for transportation to his car.

Melissa was allowed to help carry some of the lighter items, but Blake insisted on carrying everything else down to the car himself.

'I'm not going to be of much use,' she protested, 'if you insist on doing everything yourself.'

Blake laughed. 'There'll be plenty of time for you to work later, once we arrive at the house. I particularly need feminine advice on setting things out in an artistic manner. That's where you will come into your element.'

'Our tastes might not coincide,' said Melissa doubtfully. 'I've no idea what sort of things you like, or you me, for that matter,' she added practically.

'I like things to be beautiful, but at the same time homely,' he said. 'Rather like your parents' home in London.'

Melissa was surprised. 'I didn't know you'd been to my home. My parents never mentioned it.'

By now everything was loaded into his large, marooncoloured Saab and Blake had started driving out of the hospital complex, through the one-way system which meant going almost in a complete circle round the hospital from their starting point at the nurses' home.

He carried on with the conversation. 'Yes, I have had several delicious meals at your parents' house. Although I must say I didn't connect the photograph on the sideboard of a rather skinny little thing with pigtails with the rather delectable young woman I have with me today!'

Melissa couldn't stop herself from blushing. 'That wretched photograph! I'm always on at my mother to throw it away. Or at least put it out of sight.'

Blake laughed. 'She obviously treasures it, and quite rightly so.'

As they headed out of the city Melissa realised she had no idea where his house was. 'Where exactly is your new home?' she asked.

'I doubt if you would know if I told you the name of the village,' he replied. 'It's such a tiny place. It's never marked on most maps, only on the detailed Ordnance Survey ones.'

'Well, try me,' persisted Melissa.

'Dashley,' he replied, turning to her with a smile. He was right, it didn't mean a thing to her. He grinned engagingly at her puzzled expression.

'There you are, I told you that you would be none the wiser!'

The car was soon out of the city boundaries, for the hospital was situated on the northern edge of the city, only a few minutes by car from the expensive suburbs. The tree-lined avenues, where most of the hospital consultants lived, soon gave way to the dual carriageway leading on to the motorway. However, Blake turned off before the motorway and it seemed that almost immediately they were in the rolling chalk hills of the surrounding countryside.

Melissa stole a sideways glance at Blake's profile as he concentrated on the now narrow, winding country lanes. Why do you have to be so damnably attractive, she thought with a trace of bitterness, watching his stern profile. His strongly accentuated nose, iron-hard, clean-cut jaw and sculptured mouth with a hint of humour at the corners shouldn't have been attractive at all, she thought. Not if you critically analysed the features. But the combination amounted to a powerfully potent mixture, designed to turn any woman's head.

Melissa wondered if Blake knew how attractive he was, but decided not. She had to give credit where it was due and one thing he was not, was conceited. He was totally married to his work, although she had her own positive proof that he was not immune to women!

She turned her attention back to the road and saw with some surprise that they were well and truly into the countryside. Just the isolated farm house here and there, no signs of a village. She wondered how much further it was, for surely consultants were supposed to live within fifteen miles of the hospital.

Almost as if he could read her thoughts, Blake turned to her.

'I just about managed to get this house within the fifteen-mile limit,' he said. 'In fact it's only eight as the crow flies!' he grinned. 'Although I don't think the hospital administration would wear it if I moved into a house that was fifteen as the crow flies!'

Melissa laughed. 'I agree. I think even you, Mr van Reenen, would be pushing your luck a little with *that* ruse.'

'Hey, what's with the "Mr van Reenen?"' he exclaimed. 'We are off duty you know!'

Melissa blushed under his quizzical gaze. 'It just slipped out,' she said. 'Sorry, Blake.'

'That sounds better.' He reached over and squeezed her slender hand in his big strong one. 'I want you and I to be good friends,' he said. 'For your parents' sake, and mine too,' he added.

'Oh, I'm sure we shall always be good friends,' answered Melissa in a non-commital voice. But try as she might, she couldn't help feeling just a little pang of disappointment. He had seemed to emphasise the phrase 'good friends'. That was obviously what he wanted.

She had long-ago sensed that he was a lonely man. His senior position cut him off from the friendly camaraderie of the junior doctors' mess, and his unmarried status probably made it difficult for him to mix with the other consultants, most of whom had wives and hordes of children.

Why, oh why then, she thought miserably, had he

kissed her in the way he had? He had the desirable Sonia
waiting on the sidelines, ready for marriage eventually.
What more did he need? Although Sonia was too tied up
with her own career at the moment, Melissa knew that
wouldn't be for ever. She was sure Sonia was the marrying kind.

Was he impatient for love without Sonia? Did he think
that perhaps Melissa could have fitted temporarily into
the role of lover? Sexual pleasure for both of them, but
without the commitment of love. Why else would he
have kissed her like that, with a yearning hunger? She
recognised it because it had stirred the same yearning in
herself.

Pointedly she withdrew her hand from his clasp. A
friend? Yes, Blake, she thought. A lover, yes—but only
if it is me, and only me, that you want. And as she knew
that wasn't so, nor likely to be, there was no point in
being anything other than friends. The sexual attraction
that they both felt had somehow to be fended off. She
resolved there and then never to let him kiss her again.
Even though the thought of his kisses brought an
unquenchable ache within her breast.

'Yes, I would like to be *one* of your friends,' she
repeated, just to show him that she didn't want to be a
particularly special friend.

Blake flashed her a brief searching glance, then
suddenly said, 'Here we are, the village of Dashley. All
five houses plus a little Norman church!'

Melissa could hardly believe it was a village. In fact if
she had driven through it she would have merely thought
they were a few houses relatively close to each other.
But a village—never!

Blake turned the car into an overgrown drive, past a

white five bar gate that was propped open with an old cartwheel.

'The whole place needs quite a lot of work put into it,' he said unnecessarily. Melissa didn't need to be told that.

Everything was overgrown or in the process of being overgrown. As it was now spring, the greenery was sprouting profusely everywhere, brought on by the warmer temperatures. Huge banks of pale yellow primroses turned their faces to the weak sunshine. The garden seemed to stretch away into the distance on all sides of the house, which stood in an isolated position quite apart from the other houses in Dashley.

'This was once the old manor house,' said Blake, pulling the car to a halt. 'It hasn't been cared for, for these last twenty years. An old lady lived here in splendid isolation and although apparently she was very wealthy, she was also very eccentric and refused to have any work done.'

Melissa looked around her. 'It will take an army to put this right!' she said. 'Don't you find it a daunting prospect?'

Blake looked at her steadfastly. 'No, I don't,' he replied briefly. 'Would you, then?'

Melissa laughed delightedly, looking around her. 'No, I wouldn't! I'd feel like an artist let loose on a huge living canvas. It has so much potential. It could be turned into the garden of Eden.'

'But without the serpent, I hope!' remarked Blake drily. 'Come on, I'll show you over the house.' He led the way from the drive up an ancient brick path overgrown with moss, tiny wild violets peeping their purple heads out between the crevices in the bricks.

The door at the front of the house was huge and set back in an enormous Georgian porch, flanked by two sturdy Doric pillars.

'I haven't had the outside of the house painted yet,' said Blake, unlocking the door. 'It is the next thing to do, as soon as the weather becomes a little more reliable.'

As she walked through into the entrance hall, Melissa gasped. She was totally unprepared for the contrast between the unkempt outside and the beautifully restored inside.

The hall was spacious, with a tall, vaulted ceiling. She guessed that they were the original black and white ceramic tiles on the floor. The walls were painted a delicate Adam blue with the plaster cornices and decorative tracery over the inset alcoves picked out in white.

Breathlessly she turned to Blake, her eyes shining. 'It's absolutely lovely,' she said.

He regarded her for a moment, his grey eyes strangely serious. 'I'm glad it pleases you,' he said quietly. Then he led her round the rest of the house. No expense had been spared, that was quite obvious. Room after room was an aesthetic delight. The house had been modernised but none of the conveniences of modern day life noticeably intruded upon its overall beauty and serenity of atmosphere.

Blake had said very little as he showed Melissa around. It was Melissa who ran with delight from one window to another, exclaiming at the light, the colour of the room, the view. As they stood side by side in the kitchen, which somehow combined space-age technology with a country atmosphere, he said quietly,

'I had this house decorated with the girl of my dreams in mind.'

He was referring to Sonia, of course. With a sudden pain in her heart, Melissa realised that. Because Sonia was the daughter of a count and countess; she was used to elegance in the extreme. But Melissa did wonder for a fleeting moment whether she would like the isolation of the house. Sonia was used to the glamour of St Moritz and other great cities of the world, as well as the hectic life of show business. Would she like such a quiet country house?

'This place is fit for a princess,' Melissa said slowly, walking across to the wide kitchen window. Looking out she could see the primroses scattered in profusion in the garden. 'I hope it isn't too isolated though,' she murmured quietly, voicing her unspoken thoughts.

Blake was at her side in an instant. 'Too isolated?' he said, looking worried. 'I hadn't thought of that. Would that worry you a lot?'

'Oh no, it wouldn't worry me,' answered Melissa. 'It might worry some people though, like the girl of your dreams.' She was careful not to look at him as she spoke and careful not to mention Sonia by name. After all, he didn't know that Elizabeth had confided in her. She couldn't look at him, for she was afraid that her feelings for him might be transparently written all over her face. Instead, she made an exaggerated point of pulling open all the drawers and cupboards in the kitchen in a pretence of inspecting the storage space. To her surprise, Blake's mind seemed set to rest.

'It's not really isolated,' he said, a note of satisfaction in his voice.

'I know,' laughed Melissa. 'Only eight miles as the

crow flies to the County General.' They both laughed.

'Come on, we'd better start unpacking the car,' said Blake. 'The furniture vans will be arriving soon. I'm glad to see,' he added as they walked back to the car, 'that the decorators have finished and gone from the last bedroom. That means we should be able to get everything done today.'

The rest of the day was spent putting the empty house in order. Two furniture vans arrived and with the directions of Blake and Melissa a team of very willing removal men put the furniture in place. Blake told Melissa which rooms he wanted the furniture to go in and then left her to give instructions to the removal men as to the exact positioning of each piece.

'But it's your house,' Melissa had demurred. 'You may not like my way of thinking. You might have quite different ideas.'

It seemed to Melissa that Blake regarded her strangely again for a moment or two, and then his grey eyes lightened as he smiled.

'My dear girl,' he replied, 'I know that I shall be happy with whatever you do.'

So that was that! Melissa was left in her element, organising the different rooms, while Blake spent most of the day closetted away in his study sorting out his reference books into meticulous order on the bookshelves which lined the room.

They had a brief coffee-break with some sandwiches which Blake had brought with him, and invited the removal men to join them in the kitchen, which they did. After that it was back to work non-stop until about six-thirty in the evening. The removal men had left and Melissa was putting the final touches to the lounge, moving the lamps about to get the best effect in the cream and gold room. She pulled the heavy gold curtains in the big bay window together and walked back towards the doorway, surveying her handiwork.

The room looked lovely; warm and inviting, yet at the same time coolly elegant. There was something missing though, she thought looking round. What was it? Then suddenly it struck her. What the room needed was some flowers, of course. The yellow primroses would go perfectly in the shallow crystal bowl on the small round table. I'll pick them now, she thought impulsively, ignoring the fact that it was now pitch dark outside. Going to the kitchen she took a torch which she had noticed earlier, lying on the window sill.

Letting herself out of the back door she proceeded to clamber through the undergrowth towards the primroses, following the thin beam of light emitted by the torch.

It turned out to be more difficult that she had anticipated. From a distance the bank looked a smooth mound covered with primroses, but in reality it was full of deep hollows masked by the overgrowth of luxuriant greenery.

However, Melissa wasn't a girl to be easily deterred once she had made up her mind to do something, so she tenaciously clambered on. When at last she had picked the precious primroses she started back towards the house, still shining the light from the torch in front of her to help her pick her way through the tangle of greenery. Then suddenly, without warning, the light flickered and went out. Melissa swore gently under her breath and gave the torch a vigorous shake, but it was no use—it was as dead as a dodo.

It was then that she realised how stupid she had been not to leave on the kitchen lights. They would have guided her back to the house. But as it was, the kitchen was in total darkness, as was the rest of the house at the back—for hadn't she so carefully drawn the curtains?

Blindly she started stumbling back towards the dark outline of the house, the brambles clawing at her as she struggled to maintain her balance. Then the kitchen light was suddenly switched on and she heard Blake calling her name.

'I'm here!' she called, hoping that he would hear her voice through the closed door. He did. The door opened and he strode outside, staring into the darkness.

'Where the hell are you?' he called back, sounding faintly angry.

'Here!' gasped Melissa, making her way with difficulty and reaching the part of the garden illuminated by the light from the kitchen door at last.

It was just as she reached the lighted area that she put her foot down a particularly deep hole, completely covered by long grass. She would have fallen into the brambles and nettles but for Blake. In a moment he was there, his strong arms around her, saving her. For her part, Melissa kept a determined grip on her primroses as she struggled, with Blake's help, to regain her balance. But he didn't wait for her to regain it, for he swept her up in his arms, and as he did so the bitter-sweet memories of those other times came flooding back to Melissa.

He carried her into the kitchen, his lips so close to hers she could feel the intoxicating warmth of his breath on her face. She longed to feel the firm pressure of those chiselled, sensual lips on hers, to know the infinite sweetness of his mouth invading hers once more. But she

had made up her mind that she would never let him kiss
her again, and it was with an enormous effort of will
power that she forced herself to look coolly into his
hooded grey eyes, which gave no hint of his feelings, and
say,

'Thanks for rescuing me. You can put me down now,
Blake.' Her voice sounded cold and stilted in her ears,
but she marvelled that any sound came out at all, for her
throat felt constricted with an aching numbness, the
ache of tears that threatened as she fought against the
overwhelming desire to fling her arms round him.

Slowly Blake released her and lowered her gently to
the kitchen floor.

'What you actually meant was, "Don't kiss me,"
wasn't it?'

Melissa turned away abruptly, laying the primroses on
the draining board. She was totally unprepared for him
to broach the subject in such an open manner. The
silence that reigned in the kitchen at that moment almost
crackled with static electricity. Melissa knew their
awareness of each other was an almost physical thing;
pulsating emotion seemed to shoot from one to the other
like sparks.

She suddenly felt shy and awkward. Surely he knew
why he mustn't kiss her? It was a betrayal of Sonia. She
knew his affection for Sonia was genuine, so was he
really so insensitive that he didn't know what havoc his
kisses wreaked in her?

Melissa sighed. She didn't understand him, that was
for sure, but she *did* understand herself. She was not
going to weaken in her resolve not to let him kiss her
again.

'Yes,' she replied quietly, after a long silence. 'I don't

want you to kiss me. Not ever again.' She busied herself
with the primroses and continued in a toneless voice, 'I
am aware, of course, that a certain sexual attraction
seems to exist between us, but for reasons which I don't
wish to discuss, I think it is wiser for both of us to
suppress those feelings.'

Picking up the primroses, which by now she had
trimmed to the required length, her fingers having been
desperately busy all the time she had been talking to
him, feigning an air of self-composure which in reality
was far from the fact, she started towards the lounge.
But Blake's tall frame blocked her way. Desperately she
looked down at the flowers clenched tightly now in her
hand. She wasn't sure how long she could keep up the
pretence of calm if he persisted in questioning her.

'If that is the way you really feel,' he said quietly, with
an air of finality to his voice, 'I will never force my
unwelcome attentions on you again.'

He turned away abruptly to let her pass through the
doorway.

Melissa brushed past him. Even that brief contact was
a physical torment for her as she went through into
the lounge. She found it very difficult to arrange the
primroses, for her eyes were blinded with stinging,
unshed tears. Unwelcome attention, if only he knew!
But he would never know, and she could never tell
him—she was too proud. She had carefully finished the
arrangement and regained some of her composure when
Blake came into the room.

'I had prepared some steaks and a salad,' he said, 'and
a bottle of wine. I thought perhaps you would have
dinner with me here to celebrate my move into my new
home. But if you would rather not spend any more time

in my company . . .' The expression on his face was tight and closed.

Melissa impulsively went across to him and laid her hand on his sleeve. 'That would be lovely,' she said.

He turned slowly and looked at her with a faintly surprised expression on his face at the enthusiasm in her tone.

Melissa laughed gently. She felt more in command of the situation at that moment.

'Remember you said you would like us to be good friends. Well, I want that too.' She looked up at him pleadingly. 'Please Blake, can't we be just good friends?'

He looked down at her hand on the rough sleeve of his jersey. Then he looked into her green eyes hard and long. The expression in his veiled grey eyes was impossible for her to read. Then he said very slowly, almost without expression in his voice, 'If that is what you want, Melissa, that is how it will be. We shall just be good friends.'

Suddenly his expression changed and he grinned. 'It all sounds a little melodramatic, doesn't it? Like something from a soap opera on TV. Just good friends!'

Melissa laughed and the ice was broken.

'Come on,' she said, leading the way into the kitchen. 'Let's get to work with the cooking. I don't know about you, but I could eat a horse!'

'Well, I was assured by the butcher,' replied Blake in a matching bantering tone as he got the steak from the fridge, 'that this was prime fillet steak. He never mentioned anything about horse meat!'

Melissa laughed. Suddenly she felt happy, as if a great load had been lifted from her shoulders. She was glad they had at last been honest with one another. Now they both knew exactly where they stood and already the atmosphere seemed lighter. Blake seemed to have accepted it almost gladly.

Perhaps he was as disturbed and unsure of himself as I was, Melissa thought. But whatever thoughts may have passed through that handsome dark head previously, all seemed forgotten now in a hitherto unknown camaraderie which had suddenly sprung up between them.

Blake had made an understatement when he said he had just brought steak and salad with him. He had obviously been up to the house the previous day and stocked up the fridge and larder, as well as the deep freeze. He proved himself to be an excellent cook, letting Melissa help under his precise instructions.

Eventually they sat down at the solid pine table in the dining alcove of the kitchen to a meal as splendid as any that would have been served up in the most expensive restaurant in London.

Blake had insisted Melissa set out crystal wine glasses and beautiful china. A wrought-iron lamp with an orange glass shade, suspended from the wall above the table, cast a warm glow, making the cutlery and glasses winking pin-points of fire as the light cast its reflection.

They started with advocado and prawns, followed by steak *au poivre* with potatoes in their jackets and mixed salad, which was followed by fresh peaches and grapes. The whole meal was washed down with a deliciously mellow red wine.

At last Melissa leaned back contentedly.

'That was delicious, Blake,' she said, yawning. Suddenly she felt tired. 'It's been a lovely day—I've enjoyed

myself, putting your house in order. Which reminds me,'
she said suddenly. 'You haven't inspected my hard work
yet and given it your seal of approval.'

'Oh, I shall like it,' said Blake almost disinterestedly,
or so it seemed to Melissa. She couldn't help feeling a
little disappointed that he wasn't interested in looking
around the house and giving her his opinion. It seemed
that now it was done he had no further interest in it.

I suppose he is waiting for Sonia's approval, she
thought. Well, that's reasonable enough, she told herself firmly. No point in getting upset at his lack of
enthusiasm. He asked you to help, and you have, and
that is that.

Blake stood up suddenly and regarded Melissa with a
long, searching look that disconcerted her more than a
little. Against her will she felt her cheeks beginning
to burn with the tell-tale stain of pink. Then he said
abruptly,

'I must drive you back to the hospital, young lady. It is
getting very late.'

'Yes, it is,' muttered Melissa, glad that the sudden
uncomfortable silence was broken and cursing herself
for blushing so easily.

The drive back to the County General didn't take long
and it was over too soon for Melissa, who felt irrationally
that she didn't want to say goodnight to Blake. Don't be
ridiculous, she told herself as the maroon Saab pulled up
outside the nurses' home. Remember what you
agreed—just good friends.

'Thanks for all your help,' he said brusqely, reaching
across and opening the door for her.

The smell of his warm masculinity as he leaned across
her was almost too much to bear. She wanted so badly to

slide her slender arms around him and bury herself
against his warm skin. But she heard her voice saying, in
a tightly controlled manner,

'It was a pleasure, Blake. I thoroughly enjoyed it.' She
climbed out of the warmth of the car into the cold night
air and shivered.

'Get inside quickly, before you catch a chill,'
ordered Blake. 'I don't want my good friend catching
pneumonia!'

He slammed the car door shut quickly and, giving her
a brief wave of the hand, drove off without a backward
glance. Melissa stood miserably on the pathway outside
the nurses' home, watching the car as it sped down the
one-way system of the hospital road.

Was he laughing at her when he referred to her as his
good friend? She couldn't be sure.

Sighing, she turned and made her way into the building. How small her room seemed to her now as she stood
in it, remembering the exquisite, spacious house she had
just left.

The house designed for the girl of Blake's dreams; a
house fit for a princess.

CHAPTER NINE

To HER surprise, Melissa slept soundly that night. After Blake had left her with that cryptic remark and she had gone back to her room, she had felt very miserable. She wished that things could have been different, that they could be more than just good friends, as they had agreed. She wished that she had been born the beautiful blonde daughter of a count and countess, and not the red-headed daughter of a professor.

She had gone to bed with all these thoughts gyrating round in her head, expecting to lay uneasily awake for hours. But she must have dropped off soundly to sleep the moment her head hit the pillow.

She awoke, however, very early, at about five-thirty a.m. It was still dark, but dawn was beginning to break and the sun was due to rise in about half an hour. As she opened her window for a breath of fresh air she could hear the birds in the clump of trees opposite, twittering sleepily as they moved among the branches. Melissa smiled to herself. Up before the dawn chorus, she thought.

The day stretched before her, a long monotonous day of nothingness. She hadn't got anything at all planned and she didn't even know which of her friends was off duty. If she wanted to find out that would mean a series of phone calls, and even then she might not unearth anyone to spend the day with. Anyway, she felt restless. She wanted to get away from the hospital and her hospital friends. The problem was, where?

With her usual practicality born of her years of nurse training, Melissa decided that there was no point in brooding and that a hot bath and a shampoo would not only make her feel better but, who knows, she thought wryly, inspiration might even come to me in the bath, like Archimedes! Although if she ran naked down the corridors shouting eureka she had no doubt her fellow residents of the nurses' home would have no hesitation in sending for the duty psychiatrist. Melissa giggled to herself at such a ridiculous notion.

Collecting her toilet things she went across to the bathroom. As it was Sunday, most people were sleeping in late, except for those unlucky ones on duty. Anyway, she knew she would have an uninterrupted session in the bathroom, and for once could lounge in the luxury of warm, scented water without anyone hammering on the door asking for her to hurry up.

After pouring a wildly extravagant amount of expensive bath oil into the hot water, she slid into its silky, aromatic softness. Resolutely she refused to let her erring thoughts return to Blake van Reenen, and whenever they showed any signs of doing just that, which was frequently, she firmly made herself think of something else. It was as she was shampooing her hair that she suddenly knew what she would do. She would ring her mother, and if her parents were going to be at home all day, she would drive up to London to see them.

Why didn't I think of that before? she thought, roughly towelling dry her hair. I'll ring them at seven. She knew her father always got up about then to take the dog out for his morning constitutional. Having made up her mind, she fervently hoped that her parents had no other plans for the day. It was almost with trepidation that she waited for her mother's voice to answer the ringing tone.

'Hi, Mum, it's me, Melissa,' she announced.

'Darling, what a lovely surprise!' came her mother's voice over the line. Then her tone changed as she added, 'I hope there's nothing wrong, darling? This is awfully early for you to ring.'

'No, no, nothing is wrong,' Melissa hastened to re-assure her mother. 'It's just that . . .' She hesitated. 'Well, I am at a bit of a loose end and wondered if you could possibly put up with me for the day. It would only take me an hour and a half to drive up. At this time on a Sunday morning the roads will be virtually empty.'

'Why, darling, I think that's a lovely idea. You know we are always pleased to see you.' Her mother spoke very matter of factly, but Melissa knew that she had probably guessed her daughter was feeling miserable. However, to Melissa's relief, she said nothing, just carried on chatting as if it were an everyday occurrence for her daughter to ring at seven in the morning and announce she was driving to London for the day.

'Now let me see.' Melissa smiled, she could almost see her mother mentally sorting out the contents of her larder. Her mind always ran to food at the thought of visitors.

'Yes,' Mrs O'Brien said decisively, 'luckily I bought a lovely piece of pork at the butchers' yesterday. I'll do the crackling specially for you. I've plenty of vegetables, and I'll do a raspberry meringue pudding. You do still like that, don't you, dear?'

'Mum!' protested Melissa, although she knew it was

useless. 'I'm coming up to see you and Dad, not up to London just to spend the day eating!'

'I know, dear,' replied her mother absently, her mind obviously absorbed by the food. 'But you know I never think that you eat properly when you are away from home.'

When she eventually put down the telephone Melissa was smiling happily, looking forward to the day with her parents. Hurriedly she flung on a comfortable pair of jeans, a tee-shirt and a warm sweater, then she set off in her rather battered red Volkswagen Beetle for London.

As she had predicted, the roads at that time of the morning were virtually traffic-free and she made excellent time. Soon she was speeding along in the morning sunshine through the tree-lined avenues leading up to her parents' house. The houses in this area were large Victorian edifices, now lived in mostly by professional people. At last Melissa turned into the drive of her own home.

She noticed with delight that the lawns were splashed with colourful clumps of early daffodils and narcissi. Under the ornamental cherry trees in the front, which were not yet quite in blossom, were drifts of primroses.

The sight of the primroses brought a lump unexpectedly to Melissa's throat as she remembered the banks of wild primroses in that isolated garden surrounding Blake's house. Then the memory of his arms holding her after she had fallen while picking the primroses for the crystal bowl overflowed her determination to keep all thoughts of him at bay. She felt hot tears prick her eyelids at the thought of his warm, enfolding arms which she would never feel again.

The memory of his mouth so close to hers flashed

vividly before her. What made it hurt even more was
that she had to let him think she found him repellent.
She wished it had been possible for her to tell him that
she knew about Sonia, but she could never purposely
break Elizabeth's confidence. If only he had broached
the subject of Sonia she would have felt free to speak.
Yes, I would have spoken, she thought, feeling very
subdued—even though I should have had to have
swallowed every ounce of my pride to admit that I had
fallen in love with a man who didn't love me.

She wondered for the hundreth time how Blake really
did feel about her. Sometimes she almost felt that there
was hope; that he really did feel something more than
just sexual attraction, and yet . . . She always ended up
feeling as confused as ever.

Giving herself a mental shake to vanquish the un-
wanted image of Blake van Reenen, she got out of the
car and slammed the door with much more force than
was absolutely necessary to close it. Her mother came
running out of the house to meet her and flung her arms
around Melissa.

'This is a lovely, lovely surprise, darling. We are so
pleased to see you!' Keeping one arm loosely around
Melissa's shoulders as they walked up the drive, she
said, 'Your father is in the study, working as usual! Go
and interrupt him and we can all have a coffee together.'

Melissa was grateful to her mother for not trying to
probe in any way, although she knew sooner or later that
Blake van Reenen's name was bound to come up, and
then she would have to skate around the subject somehow without giving away her true feelings.

As she walked into the house with her mother, the
familiar sights and smells brought back a flood of happy

childhood memories. It always seemed to Melissa that
the old house had an all-pervading smell of lavender wax
polish. This particular morning it mingled with the
delicious smell of roasting pork and potatoes. Melissa
wrinkled her nose appreciatively as she turned to her
mother.

'Smells good,' she said simply.

Her mother beamed back at her happily. 'Go and rout
out your father and tell him coffee and biscuits are ready
in the kitchen.'

Melissa nodded and set off in the direction of her
father's study. She found him as she had expected,
surrounded by an untidy mound of papers, his head
wreathed in smoke from the pipe which was stuck in the
corner of his mouth. Melissa had always loved her
father's study, although it was not a love shared by her
mother as it was always in such a state. It was only when
her father was actually away at some foreign conference
that her mother was ever able to get in there and clean!
Professor O'Brien always maintained that if anything
was moved, even the scrappiest piece of paper, it
destroyed his train of thought. He was never happier
than when he was surrounded by books and untidy
heaps of paper.

He greeted Melissa with an absent-minded kiss and
dutifully followed his daughter into the kitchen for
coffee. It was a shabby, comfortable kitchen. Her
mother didn't go in for fancy equipment like micro-
waves, although she had recently acquired a deep
freeze, something she had resisted for years, and now
she swore by it.

As the three of them sat around the kitchen table,
drinking coffee and munching malted milk biscuits,

Melissa's mind drifted back to that beautiful kitchen in which she and Blake had dined the evening before.

Almost as if she was reading her daughter's thoughts, Mrs O'Brien said, 'You must tell us about Blake's new house. Is it truly as lovely as he has told us?' She laughed and, leaning forward, patted Melissa on the knee. 'You know, I was quite flattered. He asked my opinion about some of the colour schemes he had in mind. Which in actual fact put me in a bit of spot as I hadn't actually seen the house!'

She noticed Melissa's surprised expression because she continued, 'Yes, I was surprised too, but he insisted! I suppose it's because he hasn't got any family here of his own. He regards me as his substitute mother-figure.'

'Yes, and me as his substitute sister-figure,' said Melissa with a gaiety in her voice which did not match her feelings when she thought of Blake.

What would her mother say if she knew of the way Melissa had felt when Blake had kissed her? Hot shame flushed over her when she recalled the abandoned way her body had reacted to his powerful aura. While she had been in his arms she had craved more than just his kisses; she had longed for the fulfilment she knew his body could bring hers, ignoring that little nagging voice telling her that tomorrow would surely come, and with it remorse. He had been the one to break away every time. If he had not . . . She shuddered at the mere thought of what would surely have happened.

Only on the last occasion, when he had held her in his arms in his house, had she shown any strength of resolve and turned him away. Although she knew, deep in the secret recesses of her aching heart, that she had been but a hair's breadth away from total submission.

Her mother's voice interrupted Melissa's tortured reminiscences.

'You know, dear,' she chattered on, 'I have the feeling that Blake is contemplating marriage at last. Although I must admit that I've always regarded him as a confirmed bachelor. Still, it comes to all of them eventually,' she said, clearing up the coffee cups.

'What comes?' asked Melissa's father, puffing away at his pipe. 'Sometimes I have great difficulty in following you, dear. Your mind flits about so much. Butterfly mentality,' he mumbled.

'Love, dear,' replied his wife, not in the least perturbed. She knew that it wasn't so much that her mind flitted about, but that he usually caught up with the conversation several sentences later than everyone else, his mind usually being occupied on some scientific or medical problem.

'Love, dear,' she repeated slightly dreamily. 'Love, and with it the thoughts of marriage, have come to Blake van Reenen.'

She turned to Melissa. 'You ought to know who it is, dear. Is it someone from the hospital?'

Her bright eyes regarded Melissa searchingly. Melissa's cheeks flushed warmly. She felt uncomfortably sure that her mother had guessed her true feelings for Blake. She always had had an uncanny knack for worming the truth out of her children.

Melissa went across to the sink to escape her mother's searching gaze, and filled the washing-up bowl with warm, soapy water.

'Here, Mum, give me the coffee cups,' she said, 'while you look in the oven. I don't want my delicious pork spoiled.' Taking the coffee cups and pot from her mother she started to wash them up with studied carefulness.

'He hasn't confided in me, of course,' she said casually to her mother, picking up the conversation where she had left off. 'But from what Elizabeth, Countess Von Baden, told me while I was staying with them, I think Blake will be announcing his engagement to Sonia Von Baden very soon.'

'Really, dear?' Her mother paused, the roasting tray of pork and potatoes half in and half out of the oven. She sounded surprised. 'I had a letter from Elizabeth Von Baden only the other day and she didn't mention anything, although she did say they were coming over to England soon, and that they would be staying with Blake while they were here.' She put the heavy tray on the kitchen table and proceeded to turn the potatoes over so that they would be nicely brown and crunchy on both sides.

She paused, fork poised in mid-air. 'Come to think of it, she *did* say something about a party, but I had just assumed it would be Blake's house-warming party.'

Potatoes turned to her satisfaction, she put the roasting tray back in the oven. 'Blake has invited your father and me as well, dear. I mean to stay with him for a couple of days while Elizabeth and Edward are with him. I'm looking forward to it, and to this party. It's all a bit mysterious, now, isn't it?' she laughed. 'Is it, or is it not an engagement party? Well, we shall just have to wait and find out, won't we?'

Melissa's heart felt as if it would crack in two. Don't be ridiculous, she told herself. It is what you expected, after all. Remember, you and Blake are just good friends; that is what you agreed. She wondered vaguely why he hadn't invited her, but common sense told her that he probably hadn't had time to send out all his invitations. She was sure he would invite her, but she was not sure that she wanted to go. It would be an evening to be endured, not enjoyed.

Her mother chattered on, seemingly oblivious of Melissa's seething emotions. Ah well, she thought grimly, if I can fool my mother, I ought to be able to fool everybody else as well.

As Melissa listened to tales of her brother's latest hair-raising escapades in Nepal and of the comings and goings of her various relations whom she saw very little of, she gradually began to relax. She began to enjoy the day again, to enjoy the ordered calm, the familiar routine of the preparation of Sunday lunch, the familiar things around her. All combined, soothing her unhappy spirit. Perhaps I should leave the hosptial and work nearer home, she thought. If I didn't see Blake every day I should soon be able to forget him. She resolved to herself to think this option over very carefully when she could rationalise her thoughts where Blake was concerned.

After a late lunch, which was delicious and served with several glasses of her father's favourite German white wine, Melissa felt distinctly sleepy. So when her mother suggested she had an afternoon nap she didn't object, but acquiesced without a word.

She went up to her old room, which had not been changed since she was a child. I wonder why Mum has never had it redecorated, she mused idly, looking at the wallpaper covered with pink rosebuds and tiny blue forget-me-nots. Lying there, surrounded by familiar things, her half-forgotten childhood memories returned and she drifted off into a gentle sleep, untroubled by any thoughts of Blake van Reenen.

Her mother awoke her at about four-thirty in the afternoon with a cup of tea.

'Can't let you sleep on too long, dear,' she said briskly, 'otherwise it will be time for you to leave before you know where you are.'

Melissa stretched luxuriously. 'Mum,' she sighed, 'you don't know how much better I feel for having that nap.'

'Good,' replied her mother quietly, putting down the cup on the bedside table. As she was leaving the room she paused in the doorway. 'There's nothing wrong, is there, Melissa?'

Melissa sat up, startled. Had she been so transparent? She thought she had done very well and had kept her nagging unhappiness carefully hidden.

'No, there's nothing wrong,' she said, giving her mother a wide, reassuring grin. Her mother didn't look convinced but hesitated in the doorway.

'Don't look so worried, Mum,' said Melissa. 'I know how your imagination always works overtime.'

Her mother smiled gently. 'Yes, you are quite right where that is concerned. But one day, when you are a mother, you'll know exactly how I feel. Anyway,' she added briskly, 'I've just lit a fire in the sitting-room. Join me down there when you are ready, I'm doing a bit of knitting.' She closed the door quietly behind her and left.

Melissa was glad she had chosen not to pursue the subject, for she wasn't sure how long she could have kept up the light-hearted pretence that all was well.

Later she joined her mother and father for tea in

the sitting-room. An old-fashioned tea of crumpets and home-made scones, eaten sitting comfortably in large, shabby leather arm chairs pulled up close to the crackling flames.

The time for Melissa to leave and return to the hospital came round much too quickly and it was with regret that she at last kissed her mother and father goodbye and started the drive back to the County General.

In the morning it had seemed no distance at all, but now it was dark and had started to rain and the journey dragged on tiringly. When she eventually parked outside the nurses' home it was quite late, and as usual she had difficulty in finding a parking space. This is one advantage of having a little Beetle, she thought, squeezing into a microscopic gap.

As she entered the building she bumped into Charlie.

'Hey,' he exclaimed, 'you've been very elusive this weekend. I came knocking on your door today to see what you fancied doing. Thought perhaps we might have gone out for a meal, but then I found that you had deserted me for another.' He clasped his hands to his heart in mock-anguish. 'Me heart is fair breaking in two!'

Melissa laughed. 'Idiot,' she said affectionately. 'Actually, I've been up to London to see my parents. It's been simply ages since I've seen them. It made a lovely change.'

'Oh,' said Charlie, 'so that's where you've been! I must say, I did wonder.'

Melissa didn't reply. It was easier to let him think she had been with her parents for both Saturday and Sunday than to go into complicated explanations which were certain to be misinterpreted.

'See you on the ward round tomorrow,' shouted Charlie cheerfully as he left her. Melissa raised her hand in silent acknowledgement as the lift doors closed and she continued up to her own floor level.

Next morning she joined the assembled assortment of staff from the neuro unit waiting for the ward round to begin. They waited, chatting in the hallway at the entrance to the neurology ward, for the arrival of Blake van Reenen. Melissa took care to stand well at the back of the crowd, wanting to avoid any unnecessary contact with Blake. But even so, at the sight of his darkly handsome head as he pushed open the swing doors and strode in, her heart lurched so violently it was like a physical pain.

He appeared not to have noticed her at the back of the crowd of people, and so she was able to watch him unobserved as he started the ward round. He went first to a patient with suspected multiple sclerosis.

The patient was a young girl of nineteen and Melissa watched and listened as Blake expertly put questions to her and to one of the junior doctors he had picked out from the front of the group. There was a tacit understanding that one never mentioned the nature of the patient's illness unless the consultant had openly referred to it in front of the patient. From Blake's gentle questioning, Melissa knew that the poor girl was unaware of the disease which she almost certainly had.

Watching his face as he talked, the way his mouth moved, the slight crinkles at the corners of his eyes, the easy way his tall, muscular frame moved, Melissa acknowledged to herself that she was hopelessly in love with him. Even if she left the County General, as she had briefly considered the day before, she knew that putting miles between them couldn't blot out her feelings. She had been fooling herself to think that would have been possible. She sighed inwardly. No, there was nothing for it but to learn to live with her love, to learn to keep it well hidden and hope that in time the pain would dull into an ache. It was said that time was a great healer; she would have to wait and see. Her great testing time would come when he announced his engagement to Sonia. She just prayed she would be able to cope with it.

Melissa sighed miserably. She found it difficult to keep her mind on the ward round, in fact almost impossible, but Blake whisked them all at a brisk pace from patient to patient and she was forced to follow in the wake of his footsteps.

Don't be foolish, she tried to tell herself. There is no such thing as a broken heart. They only exist in romantic novels, they don't happen in real life. But in romantic novels, she reflected wryly, there is usually a happy ending and that doesn't happen in real life.

The ward round finished a little earlier than usual. Melissa thought Blake seemed to be in rather a hurry that morning.

'Got two craniotomies and a hypophysectomy lined up,' said Charlie glumly to Melissa, joining her as the ward round dispersed. 'That means I won't see the light of day again until tomorrow,' he grumbled. 'The consultant anaesthetist is off sick, so that only leaves me and the registrar.'

'Well, I know you are completely competent,' said Melissa. 'What are you worrying about?'

'I'm not worried about the operations,' said Charlie. 'It's just that when you are closetted in theatre, all you get in the way of sustenance is a snatched cup of coffee and a corned beef sandwich, which is usually on its last legs and curling up at the ends!'

Melissa laughed. 'The trouble with you, Charlie, is that you are always thinking of your stomach!' Waving him a cheery goodbye, she turned and started sprinting up the stairs, two at a time, back towards her own ward.

'You're in a hurry this morning.' A familiar voice behind her caused her heart to somersault crazily.

'Well, I . . .' she faltered, at a loss for words. The nearness of his presence sent the pulse in her throat fluttering wildly out of control and made the blood pound in her ears.

'I stopped by your room yesterday,' he said, his grey eyes never leaving her face, 'but you seemed to be out.'

'I *was* out,' said Melissa. 'I went up to London for the day to visit my parents.' She lifted her eyes and they were captured by his mesmerising gaze. He raised his eyebrows quizzically.

'You didn't mention that on Saturday.' It sounded almost like an accusation.

Melissa's impetuous temper flickered. 'I didn't know on Saturday,' she retorted, annoyed that he should think that he had some right to know. 'I made up my mind on the spur of the moment yesterday morning, and drove straight up to London.'

'Oh, I see,' said Blake, seeming momentarily taken aback by Melissa's swift reaction. Then he reached into the pocket of his white coat and drew out an envelope.

'This is for you,' he said. 'I intended to give it to you on Saturday, but I'm afraid I forgot. It is very remiss of me.'

Slowly Melissa took the envelope from his extended hand. This must be the invitation to the engagement party. Somehow the finality of that small envelope caused her less pain than she had anticipated. It was more of a dull, relentless ache that gnawed steadily into her heart.

CHAPTER TEN

MELISSA stared unhappily at the white envelope in her hand.

'Why, thank you, Blake,' she said, surprising herself at the steadiness of her voice.

'It's an invitation,' he said, somewhat needlessly. 'To a party.' He hesitated and seemed about to say something, then changed his mind and remained silent. An awkward silence reigned between them. Melissa was not sure whether to open the envelope then and there or put it away in her pocket. Blake broke the silence.

'It's going to be a celebration,' he said, 'for Sonia. I think everyone will be surprised.'

Oh no they won't, thought Melissa bitterly. But all she said was, 'My mother did mention something about it to me,' and put the envelope away in her pocket. She turned to go and then murmured, 'Thanks for inviting me.'

Blake seemed to hesitate again momentarily. Then he said, 'Wear something glamorous, there will be a lot of people from the world of television there.'

Melissa's laugh had an ironic ring to it. 'I doubt whether they will notice a nobody like me,' she said.

Blake looked at her sharply. 'That is a ridiculous thing to say, and not like you, Melissa.'

'Sorry,' replied Melissa shortly. 'Put it down to the fact that I got out of bed on the wrong side this morning.' She started to move away. 'Now, I really must go, or I'll have Sister breathing down my neck!'

She flashed Blake a wan smile and carried on up the stairs to the ward. Her last glimpse of him was of his tall figure standing looking after her. Was it her imagination or did he have an exasperated expression on his face? She couldn't be sure.

Once back on the ward, however, there was plenty to do and not much time for reflection on Blake's forthcoming engagement. Melissa spent her time carrying out the usual routine ward work, updating temperature and fluid charts and bathing and exercising patients.

It was not until she was off duty and back in the privacy of her own room that she opened the envelope Blake had handed her on the stairs. She had expected to see an engagement announcement, but the invitation merely requested her presence at a 'spring supper' at his home in Dashley. At the bottom of the card a quotation was printed: *Drink no longer water, but use a little wine for thy stomach's sake and thine often infirmities*. Melissa recognised its Biblical origins and her lips curved with appreciative amusement. Trust Blake to think of something clever and appropriate, she thought. It was just the sort of touch she would have expected and she knew her father would appreciate it.

In spite of the fact that she had so scornfully told Blake that no one would notice a nobody like her, Melissa spent hours scouring the shops and boutiques of the town, searching for the right outfit. She knew exactly what she wanted. Something that had that little extra and yet was within her budget. No easy matter, as she soon found out.

Ultimately she found a dress which she fell in love with

the very moment she saw it. The fact that it was way outside the price range she had set herself, she blithely ignored. Oh well, it will just have to be bread and cheese for the next two months, she thought cheerfully as she paid for the dress.

It was made of green chiffon, the filmy skirt clinging gently to her hips, then swirling out and falling into graceful handkerchief points. The top was close fitting and off the shoulder, with matching green ribbon straps. Melissa had never owned such a sophisticated dress. She had known as she turned round and looked at herself in the mirror that she just had to have it. I shan't feel a nobody in this dress, she thought, even though in reality I am.

The day of the party dawned. She hadn't seen Blake to actually talk to, other than the odd word about a patient, since the day he had given her the invitation. At first she had wondered whether perhaps he was intentionally avoiding her, but Charlie had told her that Blake had been driving himself particularly hard in theatre. Blake always undertook the long and difficult operations that Mr Wilson, the older surgeon, felt he didn't have the physical stamina for. Also, Melissa knew from Charlie that Blake used the most modern techniques, thus making possible surgery often deemed impossible by other, less skilled, surgeons.

With the work load that he had, Melissa wondered how on earth he had managed to organise the party. But then, perhaps Sonia would have been involved in the preparations. After all, it was in her honour.

In spite of herself, Melissa couldn't help feeling a little excited as she prepared herself for the evening, and when she actually had the green dress on and was ready to go she felt quite confident. She was determined to enjoy herself as much as possible, even if the man she was in love with was going to announce his engagement to another woman! Who knows, she told herself, there might be a marvellously handsome actor there who will sweep me off my feet. She grinned to herself. Anyway, even if there weren't any handsome actors, she was looking forward to seeing her parents and to meeting Edward and Elizabeth Von Baden again.

She drove herself to the party and felt just the teeniest bit intimidated when she saw all the expensive cars crammed into the drive encircling Blake's house. There were Rolls, Mercedes, Daimlers and Jaguars. They made her battered red Beetle look very sick and pathetic.

For a moment, panic engulfed Melissa. She was going to be hopelessly out of place; she wouldn't fit in all, she decided. Then her common sense prevailed. Her parents were there and Elizabeth and Edward, and Blake, of course.It was ridiculous to feel panicky! She was as good as the next person, even if her car wasn't in quite the same league. Giving her Beetle an affectionate pat, she set off up the drive.

Holding her head high, she marched determinedly up to the front door and rang the bell. She heard the bell echoing inside the house, mingling with the sound of voices and laughter. Somewhere in the background, music was playing. Blake opened the door himself.

'Melissa,' he said warmly, slipping her coat from her shoulders. 'You are late, one of the last to arrive.' He smiled. 'But welcome anyway.' His lips brushed in a warm lingering kiss against her cheek.

Don't, Blake, oh don't do that, thought Melissa,
suddenly miserable at the touch of his lips. If you knew
just what that did to me you wouldn't do it! She moved
deftly away out of his reach as he handed the coat to a
girl dressed in the uniform of a waitress.

He saw Melissa glancing at her. 'I'm afraid I had to
cheat. Not having a woman around the house, and not
having much time or talent for this sort of thing, I hired a
firm to do everything for me.'

He led her through into the large lounge and started
the introductions, at the same time adroitly removing
two glasses of champagne from a passing waiter. There
were lots of people there from the world of television,
quite a few of whom she recognised. They were noisy,
charming, witty extroverts so the conversation never
flagged.

Having made sure that she was happily mixing and
then pointing out the corner where her parents and
Elizabeth and Edward Von Baden were deep in conversation, Blake made his excuses and left her.

'The food will be served soon,' he said, 'and I must
check that everything is in order. By the way,' he added
in a low voice so that only Melissa could hear, 'you look
absolutely ravishing in that dress.' The look of
smouldering sensuality in his eyes as he spoke left
Melissa in no doubt that he meant that remark!

She felt anger flare within her. She had thought him a
more principled man than that. To regard her with a
look of blatant sexuality that chilled her to the bone and
tied her stomach up in tight little knots on the very
evening of his engagement announcement, infuriated
her.

Her green eyes flashed at him angrily, and making no

reply she deliberately made her way across to where
Sonia was standing, talking animatedly to a group of
people.

Sonia looked devastatingly chic as usual, but she
greeted Melissa with genuine pleasure, kissing her on
both cheeks in the continental fashion and introducing
her to the circle of people she was with as, 'Blake's dear
friend.'

Not dear enough, Melissa couldn't help thinking a
trifle sourly as she sipped the golden champagne. But
she kept up a witty repartee to match the conversation
around her.

The crowd in the room circulated slowly, and after
making her way through various groups of people,
introducing herself and being introduced so many times
she gave up even attempting to remember names,
Melissa saw the opportunity to join her parents.

It was with a feeling of relief that she made her way
across to join them where they stood with Elizabeth and
Edward. At least now she wouldn't have any difficulty in
remembering names.

'My dear, you look very beautiful,' said Elizabeth.
'No wonder Blake . . .' The rest of her words were
drowned by the sound of Blake's voice as he called for
silence.

Melissa stared at Elizabeth in puzzled surprise.
What on earth had she been going to say? No wonder
Blake what? Oh well, she thought resignedly, I shall
never know now. But she was still puzzling over that
cryptic beginning to Elizabeth's sentence as she slowly
turned her attention back to Blake and what he was
saying.

'Ladies and gentlemen,' Blake's ringing tones carried

as clearly across the crowded room as they did on ward rounds. Oh, Blake, thought Melissa, there is just no way that anyone can possibly ignore you, and there's no way *I'm* going to be able to ignore you. Trying to pretend that all she felt for him was friendship was going to be a heart-rending task. She wasn't even sure whether she was capable of keeping up that pretence. It was with difficulty that she dragged her wandering thoughts back to what he was saying.

'Supper is ready to be served in the adjoining room,' he was saying, 'but before we commence, can I ask you all to make sure your glasses are charged, as I have an announcement to make.'

The room was filled with the hubbub of expectant, excited conversation. The waitresses came round with chilled bottles of champagne wrapped in snowy white napkins, refilling the guests' glasses. Melissa accepted her refilled glass, a smile frozen on her lips. Her throat ached and her face felt as if it would crack in two from the effort of maintaining that frozen, empty smile. The awful moment has come, she thought desperately. It was going to be worse than she thought it would be. She could feel hot tears pricking behind her eyelids. She blinked rapidly and smiled an even brighter, wider, more brittle smile, hoping that her parents and Elizabeth and Edward wouldn't notice anything strange in her appearance. But as she glanced at them she could see that they were giving Blake all their attention, for which she was heartily thankful. Please, oh please, don't let me disgrace myself and cry, she thought desperately.

'Isn't this terribly exciting!' said her mother, standing beside her.

'Yes,' replied Melissa dully, wishing she was a million miles away at that moment.

'Well, you might sound a little more enthusiastic,' said her mother, looking at her strangely. 'Aren't you pleased for Sonia?'

Before Melissa had a chance to reply she heard Blake's voice again calling for order so that his announcement could be heard.

From the centre of the crowd of people in which she was jammed, Melissa saw Blake draw Sonia out to the middle of the room. She could hardly bear to look at her as she clung to Blake's arm, laughing excitedly and looking radiant. Then, to Melissa's surprise, she saw that Sonia was not the only person he was leading to the centre of the room. He also extracted from the crowd, and brought with him to stand by Sonia, a tall, extremely handsome blond man.

Melissa stared at the man, puzzled. His face seemed very familiar, although she couldn't think where from. Then she realised she had seen him before in a film. He was an actor, although she just couldn't think of his name.

Blake stood between the pair and put his arms around the shoulders of Sonia and the young man.

'I have a double announcement to make,' he said. Then he turned to Sonia. 'Which shall I make first?' he asked.

She giggled self-consciously and, standing on tiptoe, whispered in his ear.

Blake grinned broadly. 'I have my instructions,' he said.

Melissa turned her head away, her eyes brimming with tears that misted her vision. Sonia looked so happy it was unbearable.

'First,' he said, 'I have to announce the forthcoming marriage of Sonia Von Baden and Matthew Hoffman.' He paused momentarily, smiling, while everyone clapped. Melissa looked around. It seemed that this announcement was not unexpected by the vast majority of the people there, so what was the other thing Blake was going to announce?

Blake carried on after the clapping had died down.

'They will be married in ten days' time because almost immediately they will start work, making John Hardman's epic new film *"The Changeling"*.' Blake had to stop at this point because the whole room erupted with conversation as everyone turned to his or her neighbour, exclaiming in surprise. This news had quite obviously not been expected.

Blake had to raise his voice to make his last piece of information heard above the babble of voices.

'Just a minute!' he said. 'You haven't heard the best of it yet. This lucky pair have landed the leading roles!'

At this piece of startling news pandemonium broke out, everyone toasting Sonia and Matthew, kissing them, kissing anybody who would stand still long enough! The noise was deafening.

Melissa stood silent, quite still. She was transfixed, rooted to the spot, oblivious to the furore around her. Oblivious to the fact that people were hugging and kissing her, too, in their excitement. There was only one thought hammering through her mind, and she could not believe it. She had been quite wrong. Sonia was not going to marry Blake after all! But how could that be? She had been so certain after what Elizabeth had said, and especially after seeing Blake and Sonia together.

Now, too late, she realised she had jumped to the wrong conclusion. She had foolishly put two and two together and made five. She had spurned Blake's attentions unnecessarily.

She shuddered when she thought of the way she had been so hurtful and rude. She could have fended him off in a different way if she had so chosen to do. But she had chosen to be hurtful. She had wanted to hurt him because she had believed that he had just regarded her as a possible romantic dalliance.

Melissa sighed miserably. There was no doubt about it, she had spoilt any chance she might have had, wrecked the possibility of picking up the pieces. All these confused, chaotic thoughts raced turbulently through her mind as the crowd around her jostled, laughed and joked. She felt as if she was on a little separate island, completely alone, in the midst of a sea of people. She stood there, silent and rigid, her body racked with an aching pain. The guests around followed Blake, Sonia and Matthew into the adjoining room where supper was to be served.

Melissa bit her lip anxiously. What was she to do? What *could* she do? Nothing, she decided reluctantly. There was nothing for it but to smile and be calm and polite and say all the right things. Yes, somehow she had to do that.

She saw her mother and father being swept along in the middle of a crowd of guests towards the supper room.

'Come on, darling,' her mother shouted over her shoulder, waving frantically in Melissa's direction, as she disappeared through the doorway.

Suddenly Melissa knew she just had to get out before

the tears came. She thought she could act as if everything was just fine, but suddenly she realised that she wasn't up to acting that well, and that if she didn't make her escape soon she would break down in front of everyone. That would be just too embarrassing.

How could she explain to anyone there why she was crying? How could she say that the tears were for her own stupidity, for spoiling something that perhaps could have been. Now she would never know. Blake was a proud man. She had told him that his kisses were unwelcome, had let him think she found them easy to forget.

Even though she knew Blake was still attracted to her, he was hardly likely to come and ask for another rebuff. He was too proud for that and she couldn't blame him. Neither did she know whether she had the courage to tell him the reason she had behaved in the way she had. At that moment she was incapable of thinking clearly or logically. The only thought in her mind was to get out of that room full of people, to get away from everyone. To go somewhere where she could howl at her own folly in private.

Blinded by stinging tears, she went across the room and out into the hall. The door to Blake's study was ajar. Melissa could see the room was in darkness save for a faint warm glow from a lamp on the desk, and the flicker of flames from a small fire in the grate.

To Melissa it seemed a haven of safety and privacy for her anguish and, pushing open the door silently, she entered. Shutting the door tightly behind her she leaned against it, letting out a great shuddering sigh.

She still tried to contain her tears, knowing she would have to face the assembled company sooner or later, and

not wanting to do so with a red, blotchy face. But try as
she might she couldn't; the tears came in great, hiccup-
ing sobs, racking her slender body.

Blake's big leather armchair was pulled up by the fire,
its large shape silhouetted against the firelight. Melissa
stumbled across to it and slowly ran her fingers lovingly
across the smooth surface of the mellow leather.

'Oh Blake! Blake, I've been so stupid,' she whispered
into the darkness, voicing her thoughts out loud.

'Tell me about it,' came a deep, masculine voice she
knew so well.

Melissa gasped as a strong, warm hand came up and
grasped her fingers as they rested on the back of the
chair. Her first blind, panicky instinct was to run. To run
as far away and as fast as she possibly could. She had
thought the room to be quite empty and the shock of
finding someone there, sitting quietly in the shadows,
completely threw her. The fact that it was Blake unnerved her even more. When she had blurted out her
thoughts in her moment of anguish, she had never in a
million years expected anyone to hear her. Least of all
Blake.

She was utterly at a loss, not knowing what to say or
do. Her sobbing stopped abruptly as she drew in a sharp
breath at the shock of finding him there in the darkness.

Her inclination to run away was prevented by the fact
that Blake's hand never released his hold on hers. His
strong fingers held on to hers tightly, making flight
impossible.

Awkwardly, Melissa cleared her throat and with her
free hand attempted half-heartedly to wipe the wet tears
from her cheeks. Moving slightly to the side of the chair
she could see Blake's outline as he sat by the fire in the

semi-darkness, completely hidden from the doorway by the angle of the chair.

When she spoke her voice sounded hoarse and choked.

'Why aren't you with everybody else at supper?' Her voice faltered and petered into silence as his tall frame unfolded from the chair and he stood to face her in the darkened room.

'Why aren't you?' he countered quietly, never letting go of her hand.

Melissa's heart lurched sickeningly. There was so much she wanted to say, but at that moment the words wouldn't come. They stuck in her throat.

'Well, I . . .' Her voiced tailed off lamely. She felt a red flush creeping up her neck towards her cheeks and wondered vaguely if Blake could see it in the dim light of the room. She remained silent and was still in a half-dazed state when Blake, still holding her hand, drew her, unresisting, towards him, into the supporting circle of his arms. It was with a feeling of incredulous wonder that she felt his warm lips trace an exquisitely delicate path across her cheek-bones and follow the fine curve of her throat.

'What was it you were saying?' His voice was softly muffled, for his lips were nestling in the trembling hollow of her throat. 'Something about being so stupid? Tell me, what have you been so stupid about?'

'I can't,' gasped Melissa, half-heartedly trying to push him away. Her thoughts were whirling now in total confusion, and with his arms around her all her submerged passion was rising, threatening to engulf her. At the back of her mind was the knowledge that she ought to be able to try to explain her behaviour of the last few weeks rationally to Blake, but she knew that all the time he was holding her she was incapable of saying or doing anything.

'I can't think straight,' she muttered. 'Let me go.'

Blake laughed softly, almost triumphantly. 'Don't bother to think,' he whispered firmly. 'Just let your emotions take over; just let happen whatever will happen.'

Melissa's heart thundered so loudly in her ears she thought he surely must hear, but Blake, murmuring soft endearments, was concentrating on the hollow in her throat, where her pulse was echoing the thunder of her heart, for it fluttered wildly.

His hands gently caressed her bare shoulders, moving across her skin in an intensely sensual movement. Then his lips slid from the hollow of her throat to the curve above her collar bone. He kissed her shoulder with lingering intensity.

'Would you still prefer it if I didn't kiss you?' he asked. 'I must know. I want the truth, Melissa.' His voice took on a strong, urgent note as he suddenly thrust her away from him and held her at arm's length. 'I can't pretend to understand you, Melissa. I did think, right at the beginning, that I did. But I was wrong.'

He paused, his dark face illuminated by the flicker of fire from the coals in the fireplace. Melissa stared at him silently, still unable to speak. She could see passion etched in every line of his features. Was it truly passion for her, and for her alone? She could hardly believe it, and yet here she was in his arms, and he had been whispering soft words of endearment and his hands had made their own tactile declaration of his feelings.

Yet the feeling of unreality persisted; a little voice at

the back of her mind told her that this was all a wonderful dream and that in a moment she would wake up and that Blake, like her dream, would dissolve into emptiness. She was jolted from her trance-like state by the sound of Blake's voice, louder this time, more insistent.

'I can't pretend to understand you, Melissa. I thought at first that you felt the same about me as I felt about you. That first time I kissed you, when we were at Elizabeth's and Edward's, the way you responded so warmly, I thought . . .' He stopped and looked at her searchingly. 'But then . . .' He shook his head almost despairingly.

Melissa found her voice at last. 'Oh, I did, *I do*,' she said, unable to stop the tears coming at last. They flooded down her cheeks in an unheeded stream. 'But I thought . . .' Tears choked her voice.

Blake drew her to him urgently. 'You thought what?' His voice was rough, demanding. His fingers, which had been so gently caressing, gripped her shoulders so tightly that they hurt. 'Tell me, what was it you thought?' he demanded.

'I thought you were going to marry Sonia, and although I wanted you, I couldn't bear just to be used. I didn't want a purely physical relationship, just for your convenience. I wanted—' She paused and looked up into his face.

His dark grey eyes looked down into hers, inscrutable as ever.

Looking at him steadily, Melissa said, 'I wanted all of you, not just the sexual part.' Her mouth curved into a faint smile. 'Although I wanted that very much, too.'

Then, throwing all restraint to the winds, she flung

herself so violently into his arms that he was forced to
take a step backwards as she buried her face in his shirt
front.

'You thought that Sonia and I?' His voice had an
incredulous note to it with just a hint of laughter. 'Oh,
you little idiot! Sonia is like my sister; always has been,
always will be.'

Putting a strong, firm hand under her chin, he tipped
her tear-stained face up towards his. 'Stop crying,' he
commanded, 'you're drenching my shirt front.'

Then, slowly, with devastating sureness, his mouth
claimed hers with an insistent passion that demanded
response and brooked no refusal.

Not that he would have met with a refusal. At his
assertion that Sonia was like a sister to him, Melissa had
felt as if a great black weight of sorrow, that had hung
about her for weeks, had suddenly been lifted from her
shoulders. She felt as light as air, intoxicated with intense emotion. She surrendered willingly to his demanding kiss, sliding her arms up around his neck, her fingers
twisting in the luxurious blackness of his hair.

She felt an excited helplessness and a fierce abandon-
ment mounting inside her as his hand began to gently
knead and caress her, pulling her closer and closer to
him until she felt her pliant body beginning to fuse into
the iron muscle of his form. All the time his mouth
moved over hers in firm assurance as his kiss deepened
and the sweetness gradually changed to a desire that
became almost a physical pain, with her longing for
fulfilment.

Melissa let out a little moan. The touch of his hands
was an exquisite torment. Her body ached for closer
contact with his.

'Blake, Blake,' she heard herself whispering, over and over again, in a voice torn with passion.

'Darling, I love you so much,' he answered hoarsely. 'Too much! I think we should leave this room before . . .'

'Before you what?' teased Melissa, fluttering her eyelashes at him.

Blake laughed and, suddenly releasing her, walked over to the door and switched on the lights. 'You're a wanton hussy,' he said, 'and I don't trust myself any longer with you.'

Worried for a moment, Melissa looked into his eyes. But she needn't have worried, for his face was shining with an inner light of love. It was a love for her that Melissa had always thought would never be possible. His grey eyes were dark with suppressed passion and ablaze with a loving tenderness.

'First of all, there is something I must do,' he said formally, almost with a touch of severity in his voice. Melissa gazed at him in wonder as, taking her hand, he went down on one knee.

'Melissa O'Brien, will you marry me?' he asked, looking up at her. The overhead light threw his face into sharp relief, and glinted on the strong line of his jaw and the now gentle curve of his sculptured mouth.

Melissa looked down. 'Yes,' she said simply, lovingly tracing the outline of his jaw with the tips of her fingers.

'As soon as possible,' persisted Blake. 'I want to make you mine in every sense of the word, and I can't guarantee how long I can wait.' These last words were uttered in a voice thick with emotion.

Melissa pulled him up from his knees towards her,

searching for his mouth. 'It doesn't matter when we get married,' she whispered, her lips moving over his soflty. 'I'll marry you whenever you want.'

Blake pulled his head back and looked down at her. 'Stop kissing me,' he commanded, 'or I won't be responsible for my actions.' Melissa thrilled to the laughing, triumphant note in his voice.

With a little echoing laugh of triumph, she reached up and tried to pull him back towards her, but Blake resisted and, putting his fingers softly on her lips, shook his head.

'You wanton hussy,' he said again, with a smile in his voice. 'We will be married next week, young lady, because I insist. You've got to make an honest man of me!' Then he laughed, his eyes twinkling. 'We shall certainly give the hospital gossips something to talk about.'

Melissa laughed too, a low, deep-throated laugh, and pulled him, unresisting this time, towards her. 'Who cares?' she said. 'I'll marry you next week. Anything you say, Blake.'

'Are you always going to be so obedient?' he whispered.

'Wait and see!' was her only response before his mouth descended on hers once more.

Much, much later he raised his head and, looking at her long and slowly, said, 'Tell me just one thing.'

'Mmmm?' she murmured contentedly, still hardly able to believe that everything was real. That she was really in Blake's arms, that he really did love her.

'Why did you think I was going to marry Sonia?'

Melissa drew her head away and looked at him for a moment, a troubled look returned to her green eyes. 'It was something Elizabeth said to me when I was staying with you all at St Moritz,' she replied seriously.

Blake laughed. 'At last everything falls into place, including your strange behaviour.'

'What do you mean, my strange behaviour?' she queried.

'Well, one moment you kissed me and nearly drove me mad with desire, the next moment you totally ignored me. Then finally you told me you never wanted me to kiss you again.' He smiled. 'I can tell you, I was thoroughly confused.'

'So was I,' confessed Melissa. 'How do you think I felt when I arranged all the furniture in this house, and all the time I was thinking it was going to be for Sonia's benefit?' She kissed the gentle curve of his mouth, wondering how on earth she had ever thought that his lips were stern. 'I can tell you,' she continued, 'that it nearly broke my heart.'

'Poor Melissa, oh, my poor darling.' Blake drew her close again, kissing her so tenderly that Melissa thought she would melt from sheer ecstasy in his arms. 'I must explain to you,' he continued, pausing for a brief moment, 'why Elizabeth thought as she did. The truth is that Sonia and I encouraged it because Sonia has been secretly engaged to Matt Hoffman for some months. It had to be secret because her parents didn't approve of the idea of her marrying an actor. Happily they have now changed their minds, hence the announcement and the celebration here tonight.'

Melissa sighed contentedly. 'If only I'd known,' she said, 'we could have been together so much sooner.'

'Yes,' replied Blake gently, 'but perhaps I love you all the more for having to wait, for having to endure all those weeks of uncertainty.'

Melissa smiled back at him and, sliding her arms tightly around him, pulled herself closer to his iron-hard body. Words were not needed. He knew how she felt as she planted a hundred tiny butterfly kisses on his cheek.

'I think we ought to go back in now,' said Blake gently. 'People might begin to wonder where we are. In fact they are probably doing just that right now. We'll announce our engagement, shall we?' He didn't wait for her answer but carried on. 'Yes it's an ideal time. Your parents are here, so I'll ask your father for your hand, in the proper fashion, first.'

Melissa laughed. 'What will you do if he says no?'

Blake looked at her frowning, for a moment startled. 'Do you think he will?' he asked.

'Of course not, silly,' Melissa replied, kissing the tip of his nose. 'He'll be delighted and so will my mother. But even if they didn't approve, I'd still marry you because I'm crazy about you.'

'We're both crazy,' said Blake, giving her one last lingering kiss. 'Now, let's go back in with the rest of the guests.'

Melissa vainly tried to push her tumbled mass of hair into place. 'Do I look all right?' she asked anxiously. 'I feel very dishevelled.'

Blake laughed, a low, teasing laugh. 'You look thoroughly kissed,' he said,' he said, 'and that is precisely how you should always look. It suits you.' He brushed the end of her nose with his lips: 'Don't worry,' he said in response to Melissa's faintly anxious expression, 'you still manage to look very respectable and elegant.'

They left the study together, arms twined around one

another as they walked towards the assembled guests in the supper room.

'Do you know what I shall ask Charlie Cook to give us as a wedding present?' said Blake, a wicked twinkle in his eyes.

Mystified, Melissa shook her head.

'That green plastic frog of his,' he said. 'To remind me of the first day we met. I think I knew in my heart from the moment you let that frog fly we were set on a collision course.'

Melissa laughed at the memory. 'Yes, that first day, I remember it well. It was hardly an auspicious beginning, was it?'

'Oh, I wouldn't say that,' replied Blake seriously. 'I was always brought up to believe that green frogs inevitably popped up in the best fairy stores!'

Doctor Nurse Romances

Amongst the intense emotional pressures of modern medical life, doctors and nurses often find romance. Read about their lives and loves in the other three Doctor Nurse titles available this month.

NURSE WESTON'S NEW JOB
by Clare Lavenham

Dislike flares instantly between Nurse Louise Weston and moody paediatrician Mark Halliwell — until Louise is drawn into the doctor's unhappy household and begins to understand why he is so bad-tempered. But to fall in love with him is utter folly, surely, when she knows that Mark is a man who can never be happy?

CANDLES FOR THE SURGEON
by Helen Upshall

When blizzards disrupt Sister Peta Blair's travel plans, she's content to spend Christmas working on her children's ward — until she discovers that her troublesome new tenant, globe-trotting surgeon Ashley Reeves, is also going to be there!

THE RELUCTANT ANGEL
by Sarah Franklin

'Falling in love with Drew is like the measles — *all* the nurses catch a bout and all of them recover.' But for young Staff Nurse Sandie Masters, love for enigmatic surgeon Drew Maxwell has only one cure — and though Drew is tempted, he seems unwilling to proceed with the treatment!

Mills & Boon
the rose of romance

Mills & Boon

4 Doctor Nurse Romances
FREE

Coping with the daily tragedies and ordeals of a busy hospital, and sharing the satisfaction of a difficult job well done, people find themselves unexpectedly drawn together. Mills & Boon Doctor Nurse Romances capture perfectly the excitement, the intrigue and the emotions of modern medicine, that so often lead to overwhelming and blissful love. By becoming a regular reader of Mills & Boon Doctor Nurse Romances you can enjoy EIGHT superb new titles every two months plus a whole range of special benefits: your very own personal membership card, a free newsletter packed with recipes, competitions, bargain book offers, plus big cash savings.

**AND an Introductory FREE GIFT for YOU.
Turn over the page for details.**

**Fill in and send this coupon back today
and we'll send you
4 Introductory
Doctor Nurse Romances yours to keep**

FREE

At the same time we will reserve a
subscription to Mills & Boon
Doctor Nurse Romances for you. Every
two months you will receive the latest
8 new titles, delivered direct to your door.
You don't pay extra for delivery. Postage and
packing is always completely Free.
There is no obligation or commitment—
you receive books only for
as long as you want to.

**It's easy! Fill in the coupon below and return it to
MILLS & BOON READER SERVICE, FREEPOST, P.O. BOX 236,
CROYDON, SURREY CR9 9EL.**

**Please note: READERS IN SOUTH AFRICA write to
Mills & Boon Ltd., Postbag X3010,
Randburg 2125, S. Africa.**

- -